SHE SHALL HAVE MUSIC

PSYCHIC SEASONS
BOOK THREE

REGINA WELLING

She Shall Have Music

Copyright © 2014 by ReGina Welling

ISBN-9781500862190

Cover design by: L. Vryhof

http://reginawelling.com

First Edition

Printed in the U.S.A.

Table of Contents

CHAPTER ONE

Tender new grass spread out before her like a carpet as Amethyst curled bare toes into its lush, green fullness. A sun-warmed breeze wafted through her hair, lifting strands dyed a delicate shade of lavender to send them floating around her face. She inhaled deeply letting the earthy scent of summer refresh her as the soothing sound of a waterfall lulled her senses.

Wait a minute. Waterfall? How did that get there? She remembered choosing a guided meditation that had her walking through sunlit fields. The sound of rushing water was completely unexpected and out of place.

Frowning at the distraction, Amethyst opened her eyes, abruptly coming out of the meditation and into the present with an oath. The waterfall noise was real and coming from the laundry room.

A quick dash into the kitchen revealed a growing puddle of water spreading out from under the laundry room door; she pulled it open with a sense of dread to find an absolute gusher cascading out of the top of the machine. Lunging, the petite woman clad entirely in purple punched the button to kill the cycle and stop adding to the flood of sudsy water already swirling around her ankles.

Just what I need today—a disgusting mess, she thought, as a striped purple sock floated past. Amethyst watched the sock drift toward the floor drain under the laundry sink, then swirl around twice and sink below the layer of bubbles. And now she knew what had plugged up the drain. Next to the machine, a sodden pile of clothes, all in various shades of her signature color, humped above the water level looking like a purple mountain rising from the sea.

If the sea was made of dirty, soapy water, that is.

Blowing the hair out of her eyes in disgust she muttered to herself then waded across the room to pull the sock, its mate and two pairs of filmy—also purple—unmentionables out of the drain.

Immediately, the soapy deluge sluiced away leaving a slimy, slippery soap film on the floor.

In a state of total annoyance, Amethyst stomped into the kitchen, yanked open the broom closet door and grabbed the mop, a bucket, and a big sponge before stomping back to the laundry room.

She tried to ignore the baleful, green-eyed glare coming from the ball of ginger fur on the shelf behind the washer. Another thing she did not need today was recrimination from a fat cat. She shot him a narrow-eyed look in return.

"I'm cleaning it up, your majesty. No worries, you won't have to get your hairy toes wet." She wrinkled her nose at him. In response, he raised one hind leg and began to clean himself.

Most women would have called a repair service, but Amethyst was not most women. She prided herself on being resourceful—a real do-it-yourself type. It helped that she had a knack for understanding how mechanical things worked.

Simple logic told her whatever mechanism that triggered the machine to stop filling had failed—and that the first step was to empty the machine of water. Holding her breath, she manually selected the spin cycle to activate the pump.

It worked, the water level promptly lowered.

A quick calculation weighing the cost of a repair technician against the chance to see the inner workings of her washing machine was a no-brainer, so she booted up her laptop for a quick Internet search and found a video that showed how to troubleshoot the water level workings.

It looked simple enough, and all she needed was a screwdriver and a putty knife.

Undoing four screws to remove the control panel cover and check whether the clear vinyl pressure tube was firmly seated at the top was a breeze. Less than five minutes later, she had made visual confirmation—all good.

Back to the video and step two. Remove the front panel and check the other end of the tube.

Following instructions, she poked the putty knife into the seam and gave it a firm push to pop the first clip. With almost no resistance, that side of the front panel jolted loose. Humming to herself, she applied the tool to the second clip then lifted the entire panel right off the machine.

Just below the lip of the drum, the other end of the pressure tube appeared firmly and properly attached.

Step three—test the water level switch. That step required special tools she didn't own, so she settled for doing a visual inspection.

Frugal and conscious of the environmental need to save water, Amethyst rarely ran a load at less than full capacity, which meant the switch usually stayed at the highest setting. Maybe it was just stuck.

To test the theory, she twisted the knob. Sure enough, it turned stiffly, but after moving it through each setting several times, the motion smoothed out.

Hoping she'd found the problem, Amethyst put everything back together and turned the machine on after setting it to the lowest water level. At least if it overfilled this time, she would be able to tell before it could flood the room again.

What was that old saying about a watched pot never boiling? The same principle applied to watching a washing machine fill with water, it seemed to take forever.

When the water shut off at the proper level, she did a little happy dance and tested the next setting and finally the highest one. Each setting worked properly.

Sixty dollars saved by not calling a repair tech. Minimum. Not bad and all in time for today's appointment.

Her parents, both frugal by nature, had passed on the trait. Concern for the ecology of her planet helped her hone frugality into a skill.

Living in an underground house reduced her carbon footprint considerably since it required very little energy to heat and none at all to cool.

She'd bought the place for not much more than the cost of a good, used car. Quite a deal, really. It was a cozy home shared with Tommy the cat; an excellent roommate who kept the place mouse-free. And even if he did occasionally lose his mind and chase a housefly up the curtains, he was a champion at cuddling.

What more could a woman want?

Dread slowed his footsteps as Reid Grayson made his way along a series of empty cubicles. Well past the end of the working day on a Friday afternoon, he knew that he and the CEO, who was also the owner of the business, would be virtually alone.

He paused to mentally roll up his sleeves before knocking on the door. The corner office was situated to allow its occupant a full view of the rest of the space. Floor to ceiling glass kept scrupulously clean signaled an open door policy.

Wishing the ordeal was already over; Reid scrubbed a hand

across his face, rubbing tiredness from his eyes.

Months of agonizing had gone into this decision but this job was sucking the life out of him, and he needed to move on.

Hearing the annoyance evident in the muffled, "Come in," did nothing to change his mind. Six years was enough time spent in a job he hated.

Resolve sent a shot of steel up his spine and straightening his shoulders, Reid strode through the door to place a handwritten letter of resignation on his father's desk. Lionel Grayson gave the paper a quick glance, balled it up, and tossed it in the trash before standing and leveling a steely-eyed gaze at his only son.

"No," he said, gray eyes flashing aggressively, "I will not accept your resignation." Lionel placed both hands on his desk and leaned forward to emphasize his displeasure. Wearing a perfectly cut and fitted Italian suit over a crisp white shirt and tie, his dark hair just graying at the temples, Lionel was the perfect picture of a successful executive. With customers, he projected a calm, almost comforting presence that led to trust and ultimately to sales.

With employees, he was stern but approachable. Fair. Unless said employee was his progeny and then he was rigid and inflexible.

To avoid any semblance of nepotism, Lionel treated his son and daughter differently than the rest; they were the ones who dealt with problem clients. Whatever the snafu, it would be turned over to one of his children to handle. Consequently, both worked long hours and rarely got more than a day's vacation each year.

Reid never minded hard work; he loved the challenge of being given a problem to solve. However, the insurance business was not right for him, or he was not right for it; either way you wanted to look at it. He had no passion for the work and the constant pressure to find loopholes to avoid paying a claim went against his very nature.

When he had agreed to take this job, the knowledge that he would be helping people had been its only redeeming quality. If he had known he would spend six years trying to do the opposite, he would have done something—anything—different.

Instead, he had married young and wanted to provide for his wife, to have babies with her and to support a family. Reid preferred to give Jane the opportunity to be a stay-at-home wife and mother if that was what she wanted.

If his son found Lionel unyielding, it was only in two areas: work and Reid's aborted marriage. Lionel wanted—no—required his son to take over the company at some point and he had not approved of his daughter-in-law. Not one little bit. With her bizarre ways and penchant toward altruism, Lionel assumed she had been the one behind Reid's choice to take a job at a non-profit agency.

Lionel had used his connections to put a stop to that and to any other unsuitable job opportunity. Reid belonged in the family business and left with essentially no other choice, had come to work with and be groomed by his father. Lionel thought his son had accepted his rightful place, but now he knew better.

"Nevertheless, I'm leaving at the end of the month." Reid was adamant. Three years ago, he'd come home to find his wife gone. No note, no explanation, just the bleak, echoing emptiness she left behind in their small home. Not that he had really needed an explanation.

He knew exactly what had happened that day. She had left because he had asked her to betray herself, to deny one of the things that made her special to him and to become someone she never wanted to be. All for the sake of his job.

He missed her still.

With a sigh, he slumped in the slightly uncomfortable chair opposite his father's desk and let the misery wash over him. He hated this job and with no wife or family to provide for, his reasons for taking it no longer existed.

"Dad, I'm sorry. I would rather not fight with you over this, but I can't do it anymore. I'm leaving the agency with or without your blessing."

Lionel looked away. A mile-wide stubborn streak made him want to force the issue—to prove he knew best—just as he thought he had when he brought Reid into the agency, but he loved his son. Turning his gaze back, Lionel studied Reid, seeing his determination and admiring the younger man for standing up for himself, he capitulated.

Better to let Reid leave the company than to lose him forever.

Sighing he asked, "Who will run this place when I'm gone if you're not here? This was supposed to be my legacy."

The answer to that one seemed blindingly obvious. "Why not groom Cassie for the position? She loves the company and more importantly, she wants it. Haven't you ever noticed?"

Caught up in the notion of leaving the company to his son, Lionel had missed all the signs that his daughter was the one with the ambition, the drive to take over. Knowing the company would stay in the family went a long way toward keeping the peace.

Waving a hand to indicate that Reid should leave, Lionel said. "Go. Never mind the months' notice. Take an extended vacation or something. I'll see that you get a generous severance package."

Thankful this had gone better than expected, Reid grinned at his father who smiled back at him. "If she's still here, send your sister in on your way out. We'll see if she can sink or swim."

Reid had no doubt Cassie would swim.

Even in shark-infested waters, he would trust his sister to come out on top.

Lighter in his heart than he'd been in years, Reid stepped around the desk to shake his father's hand, then pulled the older man into a hug before walking out the door before he changed his mind.

CHAPTER TWO

Everything that he had amassed in his office over the past six years fit into a smallish cardboard box: school trophies, sales plaques, and his favorite stapler—so little to mark a life lived in this space. It surprised him to realize he would miss it a little—the familiar smell of coffee brewing in the break room, the sound of phones ringing, fax machines beeping, fingers tapping on keyboards

An unexpected sense of nostalgia settled over him as he made his way toward the lobby. As much as he knew it was time to move on, there were people he would miss seeing every day. When he next walked through these doors, it would be as the owner's son, visiting his father, not as the future CEO.

That was a promise he made to himself—here and now. This chapter of his life was over. He was thankful Lionel had capitulated so easily, but Reid was under no illusions that his father had an ulterior motive and fully expected to lure his son back into the fold at some future date.

Reid balanced the box in one hand while fishing out his car keys with the other. Once the box was stashed in his trunk, he slid into the leather seats of his only toy and gunning the engine, shot out of the parking lot.

The way he drove, it only took minutes to cover the distance between work and home while his mind raced through various possibilities. He could break out that box of video games he used to love and dive into it for a week or take the vacation his father had suggested. For the first time in his life, he was not required to be anywhere. The freedom intoxicated while it also overwhelmed.

Stepping through his front door, the emptiness on the other side slapped Reid in the face as it had every day for the past three years. In a haze of young love, he had married his high school sweetheart only days after graduation. Even now, though, he refused to admit they had been too young. With what few resources they had, Jane had managed to make a nice home for them here and after she left, he'd stayed on—partly because he was too broken to leave and partly because he thought she might come back.

Looking around at the place, memories overlaid the emptiness, and even though he knew how unhealthy it was to live with them, up until now, he could not contemplate leaving those bits of the past behind. After today, though—after leaving the company—he thought it might finally be time to move on completely. Start a new life in a new place.

The kitchen. He could still picture her there, cookbook open on the counter, steam—and sometimes smoke—wafting from the stove while she laughed at her own inability to learn how to cook.

Reid wondered where she was, what she looked like now, how she had changed.

As soon as he realized she was gone, he had begun a frantic search and found her twice. Both times, after watching her from a distance, he had found himself unable to face her. The pain had been too raw.

Jane had made her choice to leave, and now he had to live with it.

Half of a rented duplex, the single bedroom unit was small. Tiny, really. Lionel considered the home disgracefully inadequate for a man in an executive position and had voiced that particular opinion at every opportunity. Nonetheless, Reid had stayed all this time. It was the last place he remembered being truly happy.

From his vantage point by the door, he could see the entire space. A single bedroom, galley kitchen, bathroom, and a seating area Jane had eagerly decorated with flea market finds. It would probably take less than a whole day to pack everything up and move on. And he knew he should.

Instead, he put off making the decision and opened the refrigerator to see if there was anything in there worth eating. Chinese takeout. Had that been from Tuesday or Wednesday? It passed the sniff test, so he grabbed a fork and booted up his laptop, not even bothering to heat up the leftover food.

There were already emails from headhunters. Word traveled fast in the insurance business. Most of the offers were from rival companies; those he answered with a polite thanks-but-no-thanks letter. After just leaving what, for him, had been a soul-sucking position, taking another one just like it was not the plan.

An email from Cassie:

Thanks for being an idiot and getting out of my way. But seriously, I know this was your nightmare even if it's my dream come true. I'll make you proud, I promise.

Another from his friend Tyler:

Hey man, it's been awhile. I know you're busy, but we should get together. I'll be in the city one day next week, or better yet, you could take some time off and come out to the lake for a visit. You could probably use the break, and we have plenty of room.

Think about it.

Emails like these had been hitting his inbox regularly since Tyler had settled back into his hometown.

An option, maybe a good one. Take a week or so to just breathe before making any more life-altering decisions. Clear his head.

With no more deliberation, he fired off an answer:

You're right, it's been way too long, and coincidentally, I have some free time starting now if that works for you. I know it's short notice, but I could be there tomorrow.

Tyler's answer came back quickly.

Tomorrow, then. We'll be ready for you.

Okay—Reid thought—a little break and then I'll figure out where to go from here.

Tyler Kingsley was feeling that tingle he got when he was onto a good story. He had been friends with Reid Grayson since his first year with the paper. The two had met during Tyler's investigation into insurance fraud. The story, one of his first assignments, had cemented his position with the paper and his friendship with Reid.

From that day to this, he had never known the man to take a week off. Something was up.

"Hey Jules," he called out as he tracked her down in the library, "I invited my friend Reid for a visit, and he's somehow managed to clear his schedule."

For about the hundredth time that day, he knew he loved her madly when she never batted an eye at his springing a friend on her without notice.

"How long is he staying?"

"A week. Where should we put him?"

"How about the room on the other side of your office? Once we dig out some furniture, it's ready to go, and he can use the adjoining bathroom since that's already finished," she teased, "If you think you can share it."

That bathroom was the reason Tyler had chosen the suite as

his office space. White subway tiles covering the floor and walls ended just above waist level with a border of round-topped black tile above a thinner, inset border of brilliant turquoise. Above the brilliant white pedestal sink hung a spectacular art deco mirror framed in gleaming chrome and flanked by a pair of matching sconces. All three featured a sleek but angular eagle head motif. Black enameled cabinets were banded in chrome to match the towel bars, but Tyler's favorite thing in the room was the chandelier. Two levels of etched-glass globes rested in a complex series of bars attached to a set of fins that made him think of an airplane propeller. It was both cleanly sleek and ornate at the same time.

The art deco theme carried into the adjoining bedroom and the small sitting room on either side of the bath. Tyler had co-opted the sitting room for his workspace while the bedroom, with its separate entrance, remained empty.

When Tyler's fiancée Julie Hayward had inherited Hayward House from her grandmother, it had needed repairs—a new roof and windows just for a start—too expensive for her budget.

Parts of the house had been emptied and closed off to save heating costs until, spurred on by an incredible series of events, Julie and her friends had located two caches of family valuables hidden years before by her eccentric great grandfather. Now, the new roof was already finished, and the windows were being installed at a steady pace to ensure everything would be buttoned up before winter.

Bit by bit, she and Tyler were cleaning and restoring long unused rooms.

While they picked through the two large storage areas for the appropriate furniture, Julie said, "Tell me about Reid."

"He works for his dad's insurance company. Huge family expectations, there. He was married, but his wife left him, and he doesn't talk about it much. The situation really did a number on him, and all he'll say is how he screwed up the best thing in his life."

"Sounds sad." For a moment, she was quiet. "So do we tell him? I mean, what if Grams pops in unexpectedly. Or did you tell him already? After all, he's going to be visiting what amounts to a haunted house." Tyler smiled. Resident ghosts Estelle and Julius, Julie's grandmother and great grandfather, were not exactly high on the spooky scale once you got used to seeing them.

If you saw them at all. Not everyone could.

"I guess we'll have to evaluate that situation if it arises. I can't recall ever discussing our mutual belief or disbelief in the afterlife. That's not the kind of thing that comes up in casual conversation."

Julie finally located the bed frame with matching nightstands, dresser, and desk that went with that room. This particular furniture would have been among the first items sold next spring toward paying for the repairs on the roof. Now, instead, it would go back into the rooms where it belonged.

It was a sweaty bit of work to wrestle the larger pieces into place; even taken apart, the bed frame was heavy.

"Want me to clear out for the night? I could get together with the girls; tell them we've set the wedding date. After all, Christmas is only three months away. We have some planning to do if we are going to pull off a nice, intimate ceremony."

"No, don't leave. Invite them all here. I have a feeling it might do him good to be around the group." The thought had come into his head, and now Tyler was sure this was the case.

Estelle, who had violated her granddaughter's privacy yet again, concentrated on doing two things at once—remaining unseen and using her ghostly wiles to subtly influence Tyler. She felt a little uneasy about planting that suggestion in his mind, but it was necessary to move things forward as quickly as possible. Reid coming here was going to touch off some fireworks, might as well light the match sooner rather than later.

Convinced, Julie made calls to the three women she considered the next best thing to sisters. If anyone could help her plan a wedding on short notice, they could.

CHAPTER THREE

"I see a little disturbance. Right here," Amethyst reached into the tourist's aura, plucked at the strands of light until they settled back into their proper pattern, then waited for the woman to release whatever emotion was tied to the blockage she had just removed.

"My son is driving me nuts. We probably overestimated the allure of autumn foliage for a teenager. All he does is text his friends, act crabby, and sigh; I'm at my wit's end. We're headed back home the day after tomorrow, and this has been the most enjoyable part of the entire trip for me."

Amethyst smiled. This was an all too common problem. "If you don't mind a short drive, I have a suggestion that might help. Rock Ridge just put in a zip line attraction. It's not a super-fast ride but it is one of the longer ones, and for a few extra dollars, they fit riders with a helmet camera. It's popular with the teens because they get to keep the video they made. The wait can be a bit long on the weekends, but there are some perks. Decent shops and something called a Mini Spa where you can get a seated massage while you wait."

"That sounds perfect. I hope you won't take offense, but when the owner of the RV Park recommended you, I thought he was completely bonkers. And when I got here, even though he had described your place and how you could not see it from the road, I was sure this was going to be a waste of time and money, but I can't tell you how much better I feel."

Situated on the lower end of a large lake, Oakville thrived with tourist activity throughout most months of the year. The summer months through autumn were busiest followed by a lull in early winter until the snowmobile, skiing, and ice fishing seasons kicked into full swing. Early spring was nearly dead until fishing season began.

Amethyst had chosen Oakville for several reasons. Mostly because the drive home was just under two hours and the town council, sensing a trend and attempting to emulate the success of places like Sedona, had done a bit of research and determined that the edge of the lake not only rested on the crossing of two ley lines but was also home to a vortex. Once word got out, an increasing number of energy seekers found their way to the waterside village.

While Amethyst remained skeptical of energy vortexes—that was something she would have to see to believe—she also knew it would be foolish to argue against an increase in business that allowed her to make a living from her unique gift. Following on that success, she launched a series of recorded, guided meditations that she sold both online and locally. Steadily increasing sales created a nice second income.

With minimal living expenses, she was able to send money to her parents and still sock away a portion for savings. Surprised at how quickly it mounted up, she had a tidy sum stashed away already this year. Letting Julie rent the place out for fashion photo shoots only added to her nest egg.

Once the nice tourist had gone and finished for the day, she still had time for a walk down by the water before meeting her friends at Julie's house. This time, she vowed not to make any bets with Kat—well, any *more* bets with Kat. The one made when she had called to finalize arrangements for picking up the blind psychic on her way to Hayward House did not count.

Kat predicted Julie had invited them all over to announce her wedding plans and Amethyst was sure there was a new clue to the mystery of Julie's hidden family heirlooms. She stuffed a ten-dollar bill in her pocket just in case.

Amethyst glanced at her watch. If she left now, she could get to Kat's house fifteen minutes early. It had been a while so maybe it was time to ask for a Tarot reading. Walking up to the front door, she smiled as she always did when she saw the sign; Madame Zephyr, Kat's professional name and one passed down by her grandmother, did not suit her friend at all. It was such a whimsical-sounding name for Kathleen whose practicality went bone-deep.

"No, there's nothing specifically wrong, I've just been feeling a little off color lately," Amethyst explained after asking for the favor.

"So what? Blue instead of purple?" Kat teased.

"Ha-ha. Though, I suppose that phrase coming from me does have some interesting connotations," Amethyst admitted. "You're sure you don't mind?"

"Of course not." Simply dressed in a sweater over a pair of jeans, her soft, dark hair loose around her face, psychic was not the first word to come to mind when one looked at Kat. Nevertheless, she was a gifted reader and medium.

Kat reached into the cabinet and pulled out a deck of Tarot cards that she rarely used, but this one seemed appropriate to the need. This particular deck provided deeper insight into the seeker's emotional state, which is what she thought Amethyst required today.

Unwrapping the deck from its cocoon of light blue silk, she handed the cards over to Amethyst and said, "Here, you know the drill. Shuffle them, then cut the deck with your left hand. Take as much time as you need."

When the deck was back in her hand, she laid out only five

cards, face down in a simple cross pattern. Her movements were precise and habitual, ones she practiced so often she could do them in the perpetual darkness that had become her life. Kat was blind.

"The first card will define your attitude and emotions. The second will explain the reason for them. The third predicts future changes. The fourth shows the perceptions of others and the fifth card will tell what you are hiding from yourself. Are you sure you want to proceed?"

"Please—continue."

"Okay. This first card," Kat turned the card over and brushed her hand across it; her sensitive fingers reading the bumps of braille stamped along its edge as her eyes gazed blankly forward. "The Hermit, it's inverted. Normally it indicates a state where the person takes time alone to increase energy; recharge their batteries. But, inverted it means the opposite; that you have been alone too long and too much solitude is draining your energy."

"Okay, I guess we're talking relationships here?" Between clients and time spent with friends, the word solitary was not the best one to describe her current lifestyle.

"Right, and with it being one of the major arcana cards, that means the feelings are more intense, and you are at a pivot point for change. Then the next card is the Ace of Chalices which indicates a feeling of—you're not going to like this—but the best word is frailty."

"I'm small—petite, even—I'm not frail." Amethyst's voice, deep for a woman of her slight stature, dripped with scorn. Kat shook her head.

"No, it's not physical frailty but a state of defensiveness when it comes to admitting your feelings."

Well, right now, she felt a bit like a bug on a pin, Amethyst shifted in her seat. This reading was hitting a bit too close.

With Julie and Tyler paired up nicely and Gustavia finding love—she could admit it—she felt left out and honestly, just a bit jealous. The one thing she most regretted about her failed marriage was the lack of closure she had allowed herself by walking away without warning. There had been no fighting, no tearful goodbye, no slamming of the door; just some papers in the mail and it was finished.

The third card Kat flipped over was the Nine of Wands. "Well, that's an interesting card to have in this position. It signifies that in the future, you will lack protection; there will be a situation you cannot handle. At least by yourself, anyway. You will need to ask for help."

Amethyst bristled at that. She preferred being independent, being the one who helped others, not the other way around.

A tiny smile flirted across Kat's lips. She knew this was not a card Amethyst wanted to see.

The next position—the one that defined other people's perceptions—yielded the Ten of Swords. At least it was a positive card. Sort of.

Kat breathed a sigh.

"Ten of Swords means others see you as a person who plans ahead and who is far-sighted and balanced. In other words, if there is negative energy swirling around in your head over something; it is coming from you and not from others."

Her ears, their hearing sharpened from extra use, caught a faint hum of acceptance, but when Amethyst neglected to elaborate, Kat continued on to reveal the final card in the layout.

The Three of Pentacles. "And finally, the thing you choose not to see is your ability. Or, rather, your ability is the thing you undervalue most."

Kat reached across the table, and Amethyst knew the hand her friend proffered was a show of support rather than sympathy, so she met that warm grasp with one of her own. The reading had given her a lot to think about. Then with a cheeky grin, Kat said something slightly shocking. "You're not the only one who's jealous of Julie and Gustavia."

Had she said that out loud? Amethyst didn't think she had, but maybe. Still, Kat was extremely intuitive so it was no stretch to think she might have picked up on those thoughts.

"I feel like such a jerk," she admitted. "They both deserve every good thing life has to offer, and I want those things for them. But, between you and me, it's enough already."

Kat agreed, "I've never been on a date in my life—and truth be told? I even envy your failed marriage. Better to have loved and lost—or whatever the saying is—I agree with the sentiment."

"Grams, are you there?" Julie called out. She knew her grandmother was most likely to be found in or near the gazebo, so this was the first place she looked.

Used, by now, to the idea of speaking to ghosts, she didn't even flinch when Estelle appeared right in front of her.

"I'm here, no need to shout." Julie smiled at the admonition.

"Sorry. Listen, Tyler invited a friend of his to stay with us for a week. His name is Reid, and he is due to arrive any minute. We haven't decided if we should tell him about you, so please try not to freak him out." Grams tended to pop into her former home unannounced. For the sake of privacy, Julie and Tyler had tried to set some boundaries, and while Estelle was getting better at remembering to honor their wishes, there were still occasional lapses.

"Should we work out some kind of signal in case I need to talk to you? I'm getting the hang of ringing the doorbell or I could have Julius teach me how to make the lights flicker."

"If you think you can manage it, the lights would be best.

And speaking of my great grandfather, could you pass the news on to him, please?"

"Of course." Estelle appeared intrigued by the thought of having someone new in the house. "What was his name again? Do you know anything about his background?"

"His name is Reid Grayson, and Tyler has known him for several years. Grams, you know Tyler wouldn't invite anyone without being completely sure it was safe."

"Reid Grayson?" Her eyes twinkled. "Well, that's okay then."

"Do you know Reid?" Julie tried to imagine how that could be possible.

"Not personally, but I know of him. He's part of this. In fact, his coming here completes the circle."

"What circle? You've never mentioned anything about a circle. I don't understand."

"I know, and I'm sorry but..."

Julie interrupted waving her hand to indicate impatience, "Never mind; forget I asked. I should know the drill by now. You aren't allowed to explain. Is it some ghostly code of conduct where you are only able to give out just enough cryptic bits of information to be annoying? Or, did you develop a twisted sense of humor after you passed?"

"I am sorry, darling girl. Continue on with your wedding planning session, break the news that you've set the date and by the end of today, much will be clear."

"How did you know? We only decided last night."

"The ways of spirit are mysterious." Again, that twinkle.

Julie snorted. "Mysterious? Please. You're not fooling anyone; you were snooping again. We've talked about this, Tyler and I need some semblance of privacy."

An indignant Estelle replied, "I was not snooping. We are given certain bits of information, Julius and I, but only when the powers that be think we need to know."

"I'm sorry."

"And you're forgiven. Now, I must go," and with that, she faded from view.

Hoping to tell Tyler everything she had just learned, Julie turned and made her way back toward the house. She stepped onto the patio just as Lola streaked out of the woods and around the corner toward the front yard. That could only mean one thing; it was already too late, their guest had arrived. Curiosity had Julie hurrying to meet Reid.

CHAPTER FOUR

Whoever invented GPS was an absolute genius. And best of all—not having to fold it back up when you arrived at your destination. When Reid made the first turn out of Oakville, he knew he would have been hopelessly lost without that smoothly competent voice emanating from his dashboard. Proud of himself for only yelling at the device twice—he found it annoying to be told when not to turn—he whooped when he heard, "You have arrived." Tyler had not been kidding when he had said, "come to the country."

Then he rounded the final curve and let out a low whistle. Hayward House had that effect on people.

Sprawling amid a manicured expanse of lawn, the structure was a study of contrasts, a delightful, if somewhat eclectic mixture of styles. Classic Greek columns stood guard over the centrally located entrance while elaborately decorated Gothic wings complete with stained glass windows and steeply peaked roofs flanked each side. Framed by blazes of autumn—fall had come late enough this year that for the end of the first week in November, there was still a lot of color--the gleaming white house sat under an impossibly blue sky.

Tyler had also not exaggerated when he had said they had plenty of room. My entire place would fit on that porch, he thought.

Reid grabbed his bag from the back seat and barely managed ten paces before a tawny blur rounded the left corner of the house. Lola was about to make first contact. He couldn't help but grin through his unease as she ran toward him at full tilt, her powerful hind legs nearly outrunning her front ones so that her gait was uneven, graceless. He thought she looked a bit like a cartoon character—half baby giraffe, half dog—but there was nothing funny about the fact that he had nowhere to go.

Simple logic had him convinced there was no way the dog could stop in time, so he closed his eyes and braced himself for the onslaught. If those teeth were anywhere near as big as they looked from a distance, he was in deep trouble.

Beads of sweat broke out on his forehead as he heard the pounding of feet getting closer and closer. Yet, unable to help himself, he opened one eye to see the dog veer and pass him before skidding to a stop several feet away. Brown, seemingly sad eyes, at odds with her relaxed body, lolling tongue and wagging stump of a tail, met his and he felt an overpowering urge to pat himself down—make sure all his parts were intact. Not the manliest of urges, so he resisted.

A sigh of relief slipped out. The dog was not a threat. Still, her head was bigger than his was so he thought it best to keep his distance let her make the first move.

At that moment, Tyler opened the door, strolled across the porch, and pointed, "That's Lola. She's mostly harmless."

"Mostly? How comforting." He held out a hand and after shivering once. Lola took a sniff, then decided he passed muster and pressed herself against his leg as he scratched the velvety softness behind her ear.

Turning his attention back to Tyler, Reid said, "Nice place. A little subdued and understated for your tastes, I'm surprised you could settle for something so quaint," he teased.

"Well, it was the only thing available in our price range," Tyler joked. "Come inside and meet Julie. Her great grandfather was the one responsible for all this."

"Ah, a visionary."

"You have no idea." Tyler smirked as though at a private joke and led Reid into the house.

"**Hey Jules,**" Tyler called out as he heard the patio doors closing. He knew Julie had gone to the gazebo to look for Estelle. Getting the chance to know the grandmother who had raised his bride-to-be, even as a spirit was an experience to be thankful for but as much as he had come to love Estelle, the ghost had some serious boundary issues. Out of necessity, he had gotten used to her popping up at the most inopportune moments.

There was no doubt her motives were pure; Estelle loved her granddaughter and wanted nothing more than to see Julie happy before moving on to wherever it was that spirits go when their time on earth is done.

When Julie stepped around the corner, he caught her eye and with nothing more than an eloquently raised eyebrow asked if her mission had been successful. Her answer, a slight nod, went unnoticed by Reid.

"Julie, this is my friend Reid. Reid, my fiancée Julie." Tyler introduced the pair with a smile.

"Welcome. It's lovely to meet you." Julie held out a hand and greeted Reid warmly as Tyler slid an arm around her shoulders.

Reid, seeing the love radiating between them, battled the jealousy that often arose when he spent time around happy couples. Once, he had possessed that kind of love but no longer. He missed Jane. Everything about her—her sense of humor, her inability to cook, her warmth—had all been vital to his happiness.

Dragging his attention back to the present, he declined the offer of refreshment, instead opting to unpack his things.

"I'll let Tyler show you around, he knows as much about the history of this place as I do." Julie smiled ruefully. "I have some friends coming by in a little while; we have a lot planning to do. I'm sure Tyler will fill you in on that as well." She reached for Reid's hand again and squeezed it. "I hope you will be comfortable here. Now, I'll get out of your way and let you two talk." Then she left the two men alone.

A besotted grin on his face, Tyler watched her walk away. He really is happy, Reid thought, I could see why he would change careers to keep from having to leave her all the time.

"Follow me," Tyler started up the stairs, "we've put you in the room adjoining my office. It's one of my favorites." He opened the door and motioned Reid to enter the room.

The room he walked into was the epitome of art deco styling. Wallpaper in a wide black and gray stripe above simple white-paneled wainscot served as a backdrop for a large mirror in a gleaming silver frame that made him think of a bird in flight. The bed's headboard echoed the wing-like shapes, as did the dresser and a pair of nightstands.

A turquoise duvet provided just the right amount of color to keep the room from being too stark. On the wall across from the door, a stained glass window commanded his attention. Its winter scene echoed the colors in the room; white snow on a black tree below a blue sky was exquisitely wrought in glass.

Reid dropped his bag on the bed and turned to Tyler, "Nice digs."

"When Julie's great grandfather renovated the place, it seems he made a deal with a furniture designer; each room was decorated in a different style then photographed for print brochures. Julius got everything at a discount and at the time since he was a bit of a notable figure, the designer got a publicity boost. Great for his pocketbook but it made for an eclectic house. Not that I'm complaining, I like all the different styles."

At Reid's approving nod, he explained, "There are four of these windows, one for each season. The whole house was remodeled to add them. Anyway, make yourself comfortable, I've got some research going in my office, first door on the left. Come on in whenever you're ready. I'm glad you decided to come." Though he still wondered what had caused this sudden visit, Tyler suppressed his journalistic instincts and elected not to pry. Reid would fill him in when he was ready.

Tyler was off showing Reid the rest of the house and grounds when Amethyst and Kat arrived with Gustavia pulling in right behind them.

One look at Julie, her eyes glowing with anticipation and excitement, told Amethyst she would probably be kissing that tenner goodbye. Finding a new clue would not have put that look of blissful anticipation on Julie's face.

Her arm linked companionably with Kat's, Amethyst guided her friend inside. As many hours as she had spent here, Kat could probably navigate through most of the rooms without help, but it had become second nature to offer a bit of unobtrusive assistance. Besides, the physical touch helped Amethyst feel more connected.

Lola entered the room at her usual pace and seeing Fritzie, Gustavia's canine companion, immediately launched into the "Lola dance." Body twisted sideways, she leaped straight up, wiggled, then with her front legs pounced and repeated the process. She looked both joyful and ridiculous. Fritzie, a longhaired Jack Russell terrier, ran laps around the boxer as she danced, then the two of them trotted out of the room.

Shaking her head, Gustavia laughed at the spectacle then asked Julie, "What's the big news? You look like the cat that swallowed the pigeon."

"Canary," Kat corrected.

"Whatever," Gustavia replied with a wave of her hand. "My cats never once brought home a canary. Mice, frogs, snakes, and pigeons—no canaries. I don't think I've ever even seen a canary."

Conceding defeat, Kat said, "Pigeons it is."

Turning her attention back to Julie, she said, "Now, spill."

"All in good time." Julie led the way into the living room where she had already set out a tray with glasses and a pitcher of lemonade. Nearby, a stack of wedding magazines rested on the table, and without even waiting for Julie to say another word, Amethyst pulled out the ten and pressed it into Kat's hand.

"What's that for?" Gustavia raised one eyebrow.

"Just wait for Julie's news, and you'll see."

Before Julie could get a word in, Kat spoke triumphantly, "They're getting married."

"That's not news," Gustavia replied. "We were there when he proposed, remember?"

"She means they've set the date."

"December 27, right after Christmas." Julie's confirmation was followed by excited squeals and hugs of congratulation.

"Kind of short notice, is there anything else we need to know? You're not…" Amethyst rubbed her belly.

"Pregnant? No, I'm not pregnant," Julie finished the thought. "Tyler's grandfather can't travel this year—his health hasn't been good—so most of his family is coming in for the holidays—that's one reason." She began to tick them off on her fingers. "I've always dreamed of being a winter bride—that's another. When all this business with finding Great Grandfather's cache is over, Grams will have to move on. If we get married now, it will mean she can attend."

All sensible reasons.

Julie continued, "But mostly, we just want to be married. It feels like the right thing to do. We're already committed to each other; why not celebrate that at a time when his entire family will be here anyway? I love him, he loves me, it's just that simple."

Tears stung Amethyst's eyes, and as she looked over at Gustavia and Kat, it seemed she was not the only one battling the urge to blubber. She remembered that feeling of eagerness, anticipation—the overwhelming desire to belong to someone and the absolute certainty that the someone you wanted to belong to was the right one for you. Each of those feelings was still fresh within her. Even after all this time. Even after the divorce. Sometimes that feeling welled up and nearly choked the breath from her body. She missed him, plain and simple. Deciding there was no sense in raining on someone else's picnic; she forced those emotions back into the box, ruthlessly tamped down the lid, and then turned her attention back to Julie.

"So we decided to go for it, and I knew I could count on your help to pull off an intimate wedding. Here at Hayward House. Just picture it—candles and flowers everywhere. That huge room Estelle used as studio space is about the size of a small banquet hall so the caterers could set up in there."

Getting into the swing of things, Amethyst suggested, "We could use one of those heated party tents on the patio for dancing. And string fairy lights all over the gazebo. It would look spectacular against the snow."

"I've got a cousin who can play the wedding march beautifully on a harp, and my uncle owns a print shop so we can get a rush job on the invitations," Kat offered.

Julie just beamed. She had known her friends would pitch in to help her plan a beautiful wedding even with this short deadline. In the meantime, she had already asked Tyler to make one of his famous lists—guests, invitations, caterers, cake, music, and decorations. With her friend's help, she had a lot of choices to make.

The four women made quite a picture. Julie with her hair pulled back, face bare of makeup and casually dressed smiled delightedly at something Gustavia said. The fixed gaze of Kat's blind eyes still managed to be expressive; their warm blue a startling contrast to her peaches and cream complexion as she raised a graceful hand to tuck silky strands of sable hair behind her ear.

Gustavia presented a feast of color and texture; her blond hair dipping just below shoulder length dressed in a coronet of braids at the crown was interwoven with bright red and orange beads in homage to autumn; her skirt was bright yellow shading to orange at the hem.

Seeming thoughtful and slightly less animated than the others; Amethyst was fully outfitted in her signature color. Blunt-cut, chin-length hair in palest lavender matched a pair of elegantly arched eyebrows that framed crystal, green eyes. Dressed from head to toe in her favorite color, she wore comfortable jeans the color of orchids, an aubergine, striped tee and bright purple, high top Converse sneakers.

That's how Tyler and Reid found them.

CHAPTER FIVE

Amethyst looked up as Tyler walked into the room saying, "Hello ladies, I'd like to introduce you all to my friend Reid." Her eyes locked on him and the world turned over.

All the blood drained out of her face, her stomach lurched and lodged itself firmly in her throat as she tried to swallow with a mouth gone dry.

After stopping for an endless moment, her heart thumped hard against her chest, then began to beat so quickly she thought the others surely could hear it.

This couldn't be happening. What was he doing here of all places? She turned her head away to try and get the raging emotions under control before anyone noticed.

Completely oblivious to Amethyst's distress, Tyler continued, "Reid, these are our very dear friends Kat, Gustavia, and Amethyst."

Dimly through the sound of blood rushing back into her head, face flushed, Amethyst listened as Reid was greeted warmly by the others.

A jumble of thoughts arced through her mind. Had he tracked her here? And why would he bother after all this time? Three years. It felt like a lifetime had passed since she had seen his face.

No. Tyler seemed to know him, so this must be a coincidence. Some cruel twist of fate.

That face, she sneaked a peek—as familiar to her as her

own—he looked older, tired. Unexpected sadness welled up in her as memory after memory played through her mind like a film. Now she knew what it meant to have your life pass before your eyes.

Defiantly she lifted her head and said, "Hello Reid."

That voice. It was his turn to goggle and turn pale. He hadn't recognized her, she'd changed her hair—well, that was inevitable. And even her eyebrows were dyed to match—but that voice, that unmistakable voice. "Hello, Jane." Elation shot through him, but he ruthlessly controlled his face, blanking it so she wouldn't see.

"No one's called me that in years." For someone so slight, the husky, silky depth of her voice was always a surprise. It sent a chill up his spine.

Looking from one to the other, Gustavia quickly clued in to the situation. This was the ex-husband; the one Amethyst had never gotten over. Clearing her throat, she stood and gently grasped Kat's arm and pulling her to her feet, "Let's give these two a moment to catch up." And, with a series of exaggerated eye movements and the slightest of head gestures, she herded Kat and Julie toward the kitchen door.

Even though all three women had already made the mental leap, Tyler was still totally in the dark. He glanced at Reid with a questioning look only to see his friend's shocked focus still trained on Amethyst. Taking a step back toward him, Julie nearly yanked him into the kitchen, explaining in a whisper. "They used to be married."

"She's the one? Amethyst? But, she did a number on him," surprise made him speak louder than he had meant to. Tyler genuinely liked the woman, but now, he was indignant on his friend's behalf.

Voice uncharacteristically sharp, Gustavia cut in, "She was

not the only one. He asked her to stop seeing auras. To betray her gift." That part was news to Tyler. "But..."

"Butt out, Tyler," she warned, leveling her sternest gaze at him.

"We have to let them deal with their own problems."

Kat took two steps toward him, reached out, and then waited for him to bridge the distance. He did so, then taking her hand, laid it on his arm where she could feel the tension vibrating through him. "It will all work out in the end. Trust me. Its way past time that they got some closure. One way or another."

"I had no idea when I invited him here. They were already split up when I met him. This is way beyond coincidence."

Gustavia tried to keep her face solemn as she intoned, "Trust the universe," then, unable to help herself, she grinned, "to throw in a monkey wrench when it wants to."

"Don't worry; we'll all be here to pick up the pieces. For both of them." Julie could tell Tyler was bothered by the prospect of having to choose sides between two friends he cared a lot about.

Going to the door, Gustavia pressed her ear against it to try and hear what was going on in the other room. She ignored Julie's hissed, "Gustavia, stop that."

Unrepentant, Gustavia waved her away and continued listening.

In the other room, there was dead silence as Reid and Amethyst faced each other.

Even after all this time, the sight of him touched her. He'd always had a way of making her feel safe with nothing more than a look. That ability had made his betrayal even more painful, more unexpected.

Oh, she looked good. He thought he had finally put the need for her behind, but now it surged back through him; a physical

34

ache. He wanted to pull her into his arms, hear that husky laugh tremble on her lips and finally settle back into his own skin.

Reid lifted a hand, reached toward her then let it drop to his side with a sigh. Her expression was set, unreadable. With no idea what to say, he waited for her to speak first; she waited for him to do the same.

Moments passed. The silence became increasingly uncomfortable until he felt compelled to say the words that kept leaping into his head.

"I'm sorry." The words fell into the silence like a rock into water. They were so little but heartfelt and the best he had to offer.

Amethyst tried to see his aura, but could not access her ability. She was too churned up. Absently, she said, "Thank you."

Anger shot through him at her apparent indifference; he didn't see her concentrated effort to hold it together, all he saw was cold detachment.

"That's it? Just thank you—no apology for walking out on me without a word?"

To hide their trembling, she slid her hands into the pockets of her jeans. Holding on to her dignity was the only thing she could think to do in that moment of knowing how deeply they had hurt each other.

Taking a deep breath, she forced herself to remain aloof.

Time—she just needed time to process the rush of emotions she was feeling. Time and maybe a new spine. Hers felt like old, wilted celery. Celery? Really? Was her brain broken? It must be because she couldn't seem to focus on what to do or say next. Her instincts were at war.

Half of her wanted to run. Away. Fast. To crouch in the corner and protect herself from being hurt again. The other half wanted to run straight to him, leap into his arms and burrow into the safety she used to find there. Caught somewhere in the middle, she was paralyzed.

When she still didn't answer, he huffed out a breath. He could not believe this. Years apart and she had nothing to say for herself. He didn't deny his own role in the catastrophe that had been their marriage, but he was beginning to wonder if she had left because she had just stopped caring.

That he could still feel despair was a surprise.

Barely calm enough to speak, Amethyst said, "I'm sorry. I…" and rushed out of the room leaving Reid staring after her.

Nearly blinded by tears, Amethyst made her way to the kitchen. Her friends would be there, she knew, probably with a soothing cup of herbal tea. It wasn't that they were predictable; it was that they would know what she needed. And right now, she needed them—their often brutal honesty, their nurturing, their femaleness but, most of all, their understanding.

They didn't disappoint. Gustavia gave her a warm hug, Julie handed her a mug of tea and Kat lent a strong hand to hold as she sobbed out the explanation they had already worked out for themselves.

"Reid is my ex-husband."

"Duh. Figured that much out already. So what happened? Did he track you down here? Did he apologize? Do I need to go show him the business end of a hissy fit?" Gustavia asked, while still keeping a protective arm around her friend. "He didn't look too mean, I'm pretty sure I could take him."

Considering she looked like a piece of candy corn from the bright, tiered skirt to the fuzzy sweater, a full dozen strings of beads and bells hanging around her neck, the picture of Gustavia unleashing a bit of Krav Maga on Reid was enough to bring a wobbly smile to Amethyst's face. Gustavia would do it, too. Anything to protect a friend.

"Stand down, killer." The dry tone sounded more like Amethyst's normal voice as she regained some semblance of control over her rioting thoughts. "I think I'm safe enough. He's not a villain. I think I might be, though."

"I'm sorry, Amethyst. Tyler invited him. He said Reid was an old friend," Julie explained. "I'm sure he had no idea you would be here." Anything else Tyler had told her would have to remain in confidence for the time being.

"Interesting coincidence." Kat speculated.

"Coincidence," Gustavia snorted. She was a firm believer in destiny and believed coincidence was little more than a fairytale. "This was meant to be."

"It's a bit much for me right now. I can't contemplate matters of fate when I'm feeling completely freaked out." Kat gave the hand she was still holding a reassuring squeeze. She didn't need to use her psychic abilities to see Amethyst's life was about to become a lot more complicated.

"It was so unexpected, seeing him here. It's not like I've been on the run or in hiding from an abusive relationship and I don't even really blame him for what happened. He was under a lot of pressure. We were young, and both of us handled things badly." She sighed and ran a purple-tipped hand through her hair. "Seems to be a trend in our relationship. I wasn't my best today, either. I froze, and then I ran. Again."

"I don't think running will be an option after today."

"How long did you say he was staying?"

"A week. Tyler thinks something big happened because Reid took time off from work." Julie drummed her fingers on the table knowing she faced a dilemma. Tyler was the man she loved, Amethyst was family, and she really didn't want to end up stuck in the middle between them. "Do you want me to ask him to leave?"

"No, of course not." And to her surprise, she really meant it.

Seeing him again might bring some closure. Sure, it would be painful, but it was time to move on. As long as she had her circle of friends, she could face anything.

Looking at her intently, Gustavia narrowed her eyes. "Your aura just settled back into its normal patterns. I was beginning to think I was going to have to step in and help you heal it."

"Oh, I never thought of that," Kat mused, "who would we send Amethyst to if she needed help with her aura?"

"I believe I could help." Estelle appeared out of thin air.

"Grams, we talked about this." Julie slanted the ghost a look that plainly said she was annoyed. "Reid doesn't know about you, and until there has been enough time to gauge his level of open-mindedness, you can't be popping in unannounced."

"I didn't forget. I peeked first, and I promise I will only stay a minute. I just wanted to say that I am here if you need me Amethyst. Call on me anytime," and with a final look of sympathy, she faded away.

Kat broke the silence that followed, "Jane?" Her voice carried a tinge of amusement.

Rolling her eyes, Amethyst had hoped no one had caught that part, but now she admitted, "Yeah. You can probably guess what my nickname was, Plain Jane. Boring mouse brown hair, braces, and glasses. I was a nobody, a geek, until my second year of high school. The braces came off; I got contacts, cut my hair, and started experimenting with new colors. I looked better, but everyone still called me plain. Except for Reid. He wasn't one of the mean ones."

Her friends responded with murmurs of understanding.

"Then, at the beginning of senior year, a former friend outed me for seeing auras, and I became Jane Strange. Reid never called me that either, he just accepted that I was different. We talked about everything. Books and movies and life and my auras. We got closer and closer, but it took six months before he kissed me and from that moment on, we were inseparable. His parents opposed the marriage, so we eloped practically the minute I turned eighteen."

"That must have gone over well," Gustavia stated the obvious.

"Lionel, Reid's father, nearly had a heart attack when we told him. His mother was nice, though. I think she just wanted Reid to be happy."

Memories flooded back bringing with them a sense of loss. Seeing Reid again stirred up all the old feelings. The pain was no longer pushed firmly behind her, and neither was the flare of hope. What if this really was fate—thank you Gustavia for bringing that up—and what if this was their second chance?

Thinking along those lines right now was more than she could handle until she had had time to process the whole situation so Amethyst asked if they could just get back to wedding planning. What she needed right now was the distraction.

CHAPTER SIX

Tyler gave Reid a few minutes then stepped back into the room to find the man still standing in the same place with a thunderstruck expression on his face.

"Huh. I think that went well, don't you?" Reid asked Tyler, his tone was wry, but his eyes were glazed, haunted.

"Oh, man. I'm sorry. I had no idea our Amethyst was your Jane. If I'd known, I would have at least warned you. But you've been divorced for what—three years now? So, maybe it's time to move on. Seeing her now might be the best thing for that."

Reid gave a choked laugh. "Sure, that sounds entirely reasonable but here's the thing—we're not exactly divorced. I never signed the papers."

Eyes wide, Tyler asked, "Does she know that?" He was thinking this was going to complicate everything and Gustavia might get her chance at that hissy fit after all.

"Why? Is she dating someone? Is it serious?" God, he hoped not. Now that he had seen her again, jealousy burned inside him at the mere thought of her being in a serious relationship.

"No —not that I'm aware."

"Good." Relieved on several levels, Reid knew he needed to talk to Jane—Amethyst—about the state of their union.

Tyler asked, "What are you planning to do now?"

Reid walked over and slumped down on one of the overstuffed chairs, dropped his head into his hands and said,

"No idea. She's changed so much. I've had this picture in my head of the way she looked the last time I saw her. Blond, wearing slacks and a sweater; she looked like every other corporate wife."

Tyler tried to wrap his head around that one but just couldn't. Even when she had donned a business suit and wig to go on an undercover mission with Gustavia, she hadn't looked like a corporate wife. He frowned but the image just would not come. "I'm trying to picture it but I can't. Was it her idea?"

"No. It was mine," Reid admitted. "My stupid idea. I pushed her into dressing that way; I even picked out the color of the hair dye. I was so wrapped up in the idea of fitting in so I could get ahead at the company; I didn't see what I was doing to her. The worst of it is that I never even wanted that job. I knew my father was grooming me to take over for him one day and I let him. He got in my head, and then I got in hers. By the time she left, we'd both become someone else. We turned into people we were never meant to be. She just realized it sooner and had the courage to do something about it."

"Sounds like you've forgiven her." Tyler chose not to add that it sounded to him as though under all the regret, Reid was still carrying a torch for her.

"We were young. Sounds ludicrous considering it has only been what—three years? I've changed a lot during that time. Enough to finally work up the guts to hand in my resignation. As of yesterday, I'm officially unemployed."

That comment shot Tyler's eyebrows up in surprise.

"Got any plans for what to do next?"

"None—at all." Reid stood up with determination, pushed the chair back, and held a hand out to Tyler. "I'll just go up and get my stuff. Maybe when the dust settles, we can grab a beer sometime."

"Chicken." Tyler's tone was mild, teasing but there was no

41

doubt he had issued a challenge.

"Chicken? Man, that's cold. I figured since this is Julie's place she would want me to clear out. I'm not running away if that's what you're thinking."

"Funny, I didn't hear anyone ask you to leave."

"I just assumed..."

"Well, don't. I've been around these women for a few months now." Looking back, he marveled that so much had changed in just half a year. Tyler continued, "And I can tell you it doesn't pay to underestimate any one of them. Julie won't ask you to leave, but what she will do—what they all will do—is give you and Jane—Amethyst—the space and support you both need to work through...well...whatever it is you need to work through."

More than anything, Reid realized, he wanted to stay.

He needed to stay. He needed to talk to his wife. Going back into that room full of women was just about the last thing he wanted to do; he prepared himself for recriminating stares.

Reid followed Tyler into the kitchen. His defenses were up, but instead of a pack of hostile women shooting daggers at him, he found them drinking tea and chatting animatedly over several lists spread out on the table.

Apparently, he had overestimated his importance and his impact on Jane. No—he had to remember—her name was Amethyst. He had expected to see her in tears, maybe huddled in misery while her friends patted her on the shoulder and said, "There, there." Instead, he received nothing more than a brief glance as he walked in before she turned back to her friends as if nothing unusual had happened.

Debating whether to quietly withdraw or stay and confront her, he wondered if this was how a deer felt when the headlights fell on it; knowing the urgency to run but not whether to jump left or right.

If it was petty to admit he felt at least some satisfaction from seeing the redness still lingering around her eyes from crying, then he'd own it; especially considering how quickly she'd seemed to recover from their encounter while he still felt stunned.

From where he was standing, he couldn't see how badly her hands were shaking; couldn't tell her back was stiff and aching from the tension.

An awkward silence settled over the group; one that no one felt duty bound to break. Finally, after a minute that felt like two lifetimes, the two men retreated again to the living room.

"Was it just me or was that awkward?" Sarcasm dripped from Reid's tongue.

"Could have been worse. Gustavia knows Krav Maga, and she's very protective." Tyler maintained his attitude of nonchalance when Reid turned a skeptical eye on him. "I'm not kidding."

"I'll keep that in mind."

"You're staying, then?"

"Seems like the right thing to do. I need to come clean with Jane and now is as good a time as any."

"Maybe give her a day or two to settle first. Let her get used to the idea of being around you again. Then you open that particular can of worms. Not while Gustavia's around, though. She's liable to open a can of something else."

"I gotta ask, man. How did she get that name? Gustavia, I mean. It's a little different."

"Oh, she made it up for exactly that reason. You ask her sometime. Her story might surprise you."

Life settled back into as normal a pattern as it could when a person's foundations had been rocked. Over the next few days, Amethyst saw clients, worked on a few projects of her own and spent plenty of time helping with the wedding plans.

Each time she walked into Julie's house, she discreetly searched for Reid. Just to know where he was, not to check out how he looked or to see if he was checking her out, too. That would have been ridiculous. So, she absolutely never did that. Much.

She had not been surprised when his weeklong stay extended into two.

If it was hard to keep her attention on guest lists and invitations when her heart was racing because he had entered the room, she chalked it up to nerves and not any sort of attraction. What they had once had was over now even if she knew a conversation with him about it was inevitable. Maybe then, the past would finally be put to rest.

He would be leaving soon. They would say goodbye this time, and that would be the end of it. Wishing things were different wasn't rational. The intense desire to run into his arms—that would go away once he was gone. Thinking about him at all hours of the night—that would go away, too. It had to. Out of sight, out of mind.

"Earth to Amethyst." Gustavia poked her in the shoulder.

"Hey. Cut that out. I was just thinking about…"

Gustavia cut her off, "A certain someone who is not here right now? He's out in the gazebo with Tyler. They found an old power connection beneath one of the seats and wanted to check the wiring to see if it worked and if it could be updated. Finn said it needed to have the proper grounds or something."

"I wasn't thinking about him," Her defensive tone fooled no one, but they could see she needed to keep up the pretense, so all three women tried to wipe the smirks off their faces.

"Okay, then where do you stand on the big napkin debate?"
Amethyst's blank look brought another round of knowing smiles.

"Cloth or paper with a picture of Julie and Tyler on them?"

"I don't know—what does Julie want?" She turned to Julie. "What do you want?"

"Cloth for the dinner, paper for the cake, but not with our picture. Just our names and the date."

"Well, that's settled and with no need for debate," Kat said. "Now for the music, this is short notice for finding a band not already booked for the holidays, but I might have a solution. My cousin, the harpist, also plays in a string quartet. They're all in high school, but they're very talented, and I know they'd love the chance to play for you."

"That could work during the dinner, and then I think Tyler has a line on a deejay for dancing. Could they come and do an audition?"

Kat grinned and reached back for the handbag she had hung on the back of the chair. She pulled out a CD and held it toward Julie. "They heard me telling mom about the wedding and put together a demo. It's not professionally recorded or anything, but they were so excited they made me promise to ask if you could at least listen to it." Wedding planning was a visual task, which minimized her contribution but her friends always included her in everything, so she was happy to have something to offer.

"I'll give it a listen and let you know." Julie accepted the disk and laid it aside before pulling out a book of invitation samples. "Kat's uncle does exquisite work, and he says he can do the napkins to match."

Amethyst pulled the book over and began looking through the pages. "These are gorgeous, and it's so much nicer to be able to see them in person rather than on a computer screen. I love this textured card stock, it has such a nice feel to it." She brushed a fingertip over the paper.

"If I have the guest list ready by the time I order, they have a calligrapher on staff who will address the envelopes. Take a look at her samples in the back, they're just beautiful."

"Do you have the guest list ready?"

Julie exchanged a glance with Gustavia. "I do, and you should know that Reid will be coming to the wedding."

"Of course, I expected that. I'm fine with it." There was more though, she could tell by the look on their faces.

"He's going to be filling in for Tyler's brother who won't be able to make it back in time for the wedding. As Best Man."

Well, that complicated things. He would be around a little more than she'd planned. A surge of hope shot through her until she reined it back in.

"I'll make it work, no worries."

"Yes, I'm sure you will." Gustavia's remark was met with wrinkled-nose scorn.

"Moving on." Estelle threw the two women a quelling glance, though the surprise of her presence was enough to accomplish that goal anyway.

"Sneaking up on us again, Grams?" Julie asked, but she was glad her grandmother was getting the chance to take a small part in the wedding plans.

The belated dinging of the doorbell sounded, and the lights dimmed. Estelle had agreed to give some kind of warning sign before she appeared but was abysmal at remembering to do so.

"Better late than never." Julie rolled her eyes, and Amethyst snorted out a laugh.

"I would like to ask Kathleen for a favor." Estelle turned toward the blind psychic. "Do you think it would be possible for me to accompany you when you girls go dress shopping?" She was asking Kat to channel her when the time came. "I'd like to be able to touch the dress and feel more a part of things, but I understand if you'd prefer not."

Since any channeling of Estelle gave Kat the ability to see, this was a mutually beneficial opportunity. She would have the chance to participate fully. "Yes, of course."

"Thank you, dear." Estelle intended to help the girl regain her sight before she went into the light. All Kat needed to do was to fully release her fear of seeing spirit—something she was already well on her way toward doing—and her vision should return since there was no physical reason for her blindness.

"Now, show me those invitations quickly before I have to go again."

CHAPTER SEVEN

Something drew Logan Ellis back to Oakville. Something just as irresistible as the fiery death a moth endured when called to the flame and he was just as likely to get burned—the force inside him would not rest until he returned.

In his lucid moments, he knew he should run. Just put Julie and the past in his rearview mirror, hit the beach, rest up and get his mojo back. Unfortunately, his lucid moments were few and fleeting. Instead, he found himself squatting on an abandoned farm in an area that his former, saner self would have called "Oakville adjacent."

Today, the tiny spark of sanity he could claim only managed to burn back the shadows but not banish them completely. It surfaced now and eyes darting from side to side, he took stock of his situation.

Colder nights and living rough had thinned him; carved away at flesh and bone as he shivered in the dark too far gone some nights to even search for warmth. He tore through the house looking for anything warmer to wear, any shred of clothing left behind. A few pieces of furniture remained in the old place, and he was glad to see at least one bed with a lumpy, stained mattress, but neither of the two cast-off dressers held a single article of clothing and the closets were empty.

He opened every door, every cabinet in the place before finding a set of narrow stairs leading to the attic where he hit pay dirt. Forgotten boxes damaged by the leaky roof had burst and spewed their contents. Kicking aside piles of old papers, he found a stained quilt and several articles of damp clothing.

The quilt, in a wedding ring pattern, smelled ripely of old musty cloth but it was dry and warm, so he tossed it over his shoulders like a cape, then quickly sorted through the clothes. Jeans that would be at least an inch too long on him, a couple sweatshirts and at the very bottom, a fleece lined jacket.

He carried them all downstairs and out into the sunny yard where he spread them over the porch rails to dry. Maybe the sun would burn off some of the smell.

Once this chore was done, Logan became more aware of the world around him. Oak trees, the town's namesakes, surrounded overgrown fields of frost-browned grass. The trees were vividly dressed in shades of russet, yellow, and green. How much time had he lost? The last he remembered, he had been sweating through hot summer nights in the woods.

Logan searched his memory, but all that came back to him were snippets—brief flashes of time. A big dog coming at him with teeth bared, he clutched his arm and found the wound had healed to an angry red scar. He remembered the satisfying sound of a baseball bat crashing through glass, but mostly there were long, blank spaces where he had been lost to himself and to the world.

Lifting his face to the sun, he absorbed its light and heat and wished he never needed to go back into the dark. Stomach churning with hunger, he searched for something edible. It was a farm and farmers tended to plant things; maybe a few perennial vegetables had survived the killing frost.

He took one circuit around the house and found a small kitchen garden that the wilderness was already in the process of reclaiming. To his relief, that worked in his favor when he found a patch of hardy kale that had been overgrown by thick grass. The grass had taken the brunt of any frost damage leaving much of the kale alive and ready to eat.

This success was followed by the discovery of some small, pinkish onions and a row of forgotten carrots. He pulled several of the carrots and wiped them on the grass. With most of the dirt removed, Logan ate them in large, hungry bites that hit his empty belly and made it gurgle with the need for more. Still, they were sweet and earthy. Nothing had ever tasted so good. Pungent raw onions wrapped in kale followed the carrots until he finally had his fill.

Sated, tired, and finally warm, he stumbled back inside and made his way to the bedroom. Sinking into the old mattress and hoping he would wake up himself again, Logan dropped over the edge of sleep.

And back into darkness.

"He's back." Estelle's exclamation came just before the faint ringing of the doorbell as she abruptly appeared in the center of the room. The lights flickered.

"Grams, we talked about this." Julie shook her head then chanced a cautious glance at Reid. She took in his pale face and shocked expression. Nothing to be done about it now. Noting Amethyst's amused expression, Julie quirked an eyebrow at her before assuring Reid that his eyes had not deceived him.

"Reid, I'd like you to meet my dearly departed grandmother, Estelle." Not much sense trying to dance around the truth, he had seen what he had seen, and they might as well just deal with it.

"But she...she just..." he trailed off as he tried to make sense of what he had seen. The woman had just appeared there like a ghost. Then his brain caught up. "Wait a minute, did you say dearly departed? But I don't believe in ghosts."

With a wicked twinkle in her eye, Estelle informed him,

"That's okay, young man. We believe in you."

He speared a look at Amethyst. "Did you know about this?"

"Naturally," she treated him to the first genuine smile he had seen from her since his arrival. His brain registered that fact in addition to noticing she did not attempt to hide her delight at his obvious distress. The smile remained even as she pulled a ten-dollar bill out of her pocket and handed it over to Kat. "Another day and I'd have had you on that one." Instead, she had lost yet another bet to the psychic.

Turning to Reid, Amethyst said, "Not to worry, she's friendly, like Caspar." Her words were meant to be reassuring, but he got the feeling she was mocking him. At least a little, anyway. He rolled his eyes at her.

"Nice to meet you," he mumbled as he glared daggers at Tyler. "You could have warned me." Then he fell silent.

"Didn't you hear me? I said he's back." Now that the introductions were over, Estelle's agitation increased. "What are you going to do to keep my girls safe?" She demanded an answer from Tyler.

When Julius appeared next to Estelle, Reid only shook his head then sat back to rest one crossed leg over the other. It was hard to sustain a state of shock when everyone around him seemed comfortable in the presence of these two—well—presences.

Julie's ex, once the consummate con man had targeted her in an attempt to wrest away control of Hayward House and the property around it. Fortunately, his plan to sell the acreage to a developer had been foiled by a little judicious sleuthing on the part of Amethyst and Gustavia. The pair of them, dressed up in thrift store business attire, had infiltrated Logan's office and uncovered the plot.

"How did you find him? I thought he had learned how to shield himself from you." Amethyst asked Julius.

"He did, but for a few hours today, the blinders came off, and his mind was clear…" Julius broke off, his expression troubled.

Amethyst read his aura and saw the colors she usually associated with compassion mixed in with the anger that Julius most often displayed when talking about Logan. Odd, she thought, he feels sorry for the man.

Gently she said, "You're feeling just a bit sorry for him now. What's changed?"

Julius scowled at her, "Very perceptive, young woman. Don't get me wrong, that boy has done horrible things, and he deserves to be punished for them. His intentions have never been good but whatever evil he called to himself because of his actions—no one deserves to have something like that riding him."

"You think we have to help him, don't you?" Gustavia broke in, "After all he's done, you want to help him." Since she had taken the brunt of his most recent crime spree, Gustavia's compassion for Logan was completely non-existent.

Julius sighed. He understood her reservations.

"Yes, young Gustavia, I think we may have to help him in order to catch him. Your brother is doing an admirable job making a legal case against Logan, but you must see that he has to follow procedure, go through channels. It's keeping him two steps behind, and we need to be more proactive if we are going to end this situation."

Gustavia's aura darkened, swirling dangerously. Amethyst touched her arm and did what she could to diffuse the wash of negativity.

"He's not suggesting we adopt the idiot, Gustavia—just that we level the playing field by getting rid of any outside influences."

Nodding his agreement, Julius said, "Exactly right."

This appeased Gustavia enough that her aura settled back to normal leaving Amethyst free to glance over at Reid's. His was still a whirl of unsettled color but, for once, she battled her instincts to help and left him alone. Touching his aura right now would feel a bit too presumptuous. Too intimate. Too good.

He'd have to fend for himself this time.

She turned back to Julius and asked the question everyone was thinking, "Do you have a plan?"

He dropped his head. Amethyst watched his aura take on a tinge of uncertainty.

"I have ideas," he almost mumbled the words then raised his head, his gaze searching as he looked at her for a long moment.

"What? Do I have something stuck in my teeth?" She tried to joke, but it fell flat.

"How far are you willing to go to keep your friends safe? How deeply would you explore your abilities?"

The question struck her as odd because her ability could hardly be described as defensive. Her mind generated an image of herself in tights and a purple cape leaping into the fray and plucking away dark blobs of light from an attacker's aura. Yeah, right—she thought—Aura Woman will save the day—and Julius could be her sidekick, Captain Crazypants.

"I'd do whatever it takes, not that I'm convinced anything about aura reading would help keep them safe." She was emphatic and thankful that no one in the room was a mind reader. Oh, please let Kat not be a mind reader. Embarrassment at even the mere thought that someone could read her thoughts sent a blush of pink across Amethyst's cheeks.

A slight nod then, looking around the room, Julius spotted Reid.

"Is this your young man?" He asked Amethyst.

Red-faced and stammering she replied, "Um. It's

complicated. He was once, but now he's just—well—he's not."

Was Julius smirking at her? Amethyst narrowed her eyes and pinned him with a glare, which did absolutely nothing to change his expression.

"Be that as it may, I approve. Do not let her slip away again, boy. She's a keeper."

Amethyst didn't think it was possible to blush harder but was proved wrong. A glance around the room didn't help much; every one of her friends appeared to agree with Julius.

Struggling to recover her normally dry sense of humor, she said, "Yeah, I guess I'm the catch of the day. Can we move on now?"

Instead, Julius cocked his head and looked appraisingly at Reid who now felt like a side of beef at a chef's convention. "Good heart, decent intellect, and enough strength and sensitivity to become both conduit and protector. He'll do."

If she had been embarrassed before, now Amethyst wished the floor would just open up and swallow her whole. "You're making assumptions, old man."

Knowing Julius tended to be blunt and lacked the least bit of social awareness; Estelle cheerfully stepped in to smooth things over. She rested a hand on his arm and whispered loudly, "Let them come to it in their own time."

"Fine." He looked from Amethyst to Reid and cautioned them, "Just be ready to play your part when the time comes. And don't be fools about it, either."

Regaining his serious demeanor, Julius stated, "You will all need to be on your guard because I am going to be away for a while. There is an errand I must complete. An important one. Stick together, it might be a cliché, but there is safety in numbers." Nodding to the room, he faded abruptly from view.

Estelle said her goodbyes, gave Reid a cheery wink through the worry that still showed on her face, and did the same.

Breaking the silence that had descended on the room, Reid nearly shouted, "What just happened?" He looked around to see a variety of expressions from grins to concerned looks turned his way.

At last, Finn, who had remained largely silent until now, offered dryly, "Stick around. It gets less freaky after the fourth or fifth time. Pretty soon, hanging out with ghosts will seem ordinary." Gustavia mockingly punched him in the arm.

When Julie spoke, her tone was apologetic, "I'm sorry, Reid. I warned her about just popping in like that, but it clearly didn't do any good. She tends to act first and think later. I'm sure you have questions." She nodded to indicate he should ask them.

A hundred thoughts chased each other through his mind at such a rapid pace that he failed to isolate any one of them.

"I'm sure I do, but I can't seem to formulate any at the moment. Maybe you should just tell me what kind of mess I've blundered my way into," and he sat back, waiting.

Gustavia began, "It all started when I took Julie to see Kat for a psychic reading as an engagement gift. Her grandmother and great grandfather came through—you've just met them for yourselves, and that started us off on the treasure hunt."

Tyler added, "That's where I came in. My grandfather, the historian, had some notes about Hayward House and Julie's family, so I brought them over and got caught up in the search and in Julie, too. But she was engaged to Logan, a world-class creep who turned out to be a con man."

Amethyst took up the story. "We figured out his plan by going incognito and infiltrating his office. His boss gave me a pitch about buying a condo on this very property. Logan had negotiated the sale of Julie's house and the land without her knowledge and was trying to get her to sign over full control of it upon their marriage. She wouldn't have been able to stop him."

"So, I dumped him…" Julie began.

"Quite spectacularly, I might add," Gustavia cut in.

"And he decided to get revenge," Julie continued.

"Mostly on Gustavia, because he blames her for Julie catching on to his plan and because he thinks she is more vulnerable. A few weeks ago, he cut her brake lines and caused an accident," Finn said. The dark and brooding look on his face spoke of his desire to cause Logan some major bodily damage.

"We could have been killed. I think he was hoping for that. Julius thinks he is—possessed isn't the right word, but it's the closest description we can come up with—by a ghost, possibly one of his ancestors." Kat explained.

Incredulous, Reid looked at the faces around him. None of them was joking and considering he had just seen two ghosts, he guessed he might as well believe. "A treasure hunt?"

Gustavia hooted, "Ghosts, danger, and intrigue—yet every time it's the treasure they pick up on first. Men." A wide smile diffused her mocking tone.

"Treasure hunts and nubile women finding us irresistible—two things every man dreams of." All four women rolled their eyes while the other two men nodded in agreement.

"It's just how we're wired; tell me more about the treasure." Still, in the back of his mind, Reid brooded over the question Julius had asked Amethyst. How far was she willing to go to keep her friends safe? It sounded like there was some type of risk involved and until he knew what that risk might be, he was sticking around. First chance, he'd have to talk to Julie and Tyler about extending his visit again. In the meantime, though, there was a story about treasure he was dying to hear.

Before that, though, he felt compelled to ask, "Is that it? Are there any more secrets I should know about?"

Amethyst ticked off the points for him, "Ghosts, family

legacy, crazy and possibly possessed con man out for revenge, Kat's has prodigious psychic abilities—Oh, Gustavia's father is Senator Roman and her name used to be Eloise. I'd say that about covers it." Except for the fact, she still had feelings for him.

"Okay, then. Tell me about the treasure."

An hour or so later, after crawling into the hidden library nook and getting Finn to show him how they had lowered the chandelier, Reid had also learned that the next quest probably involved the spectacular stained glass window in the room he currently occupied.

He insisted they all inspect it for clues.

"We should have asked Julius about the key before he left on his mysterious mission," Gustavia stated the obvious.

"He hasn't left yet. I can still feel him nearby." Kat explained, "Let me see if I can get him back."

She concentrated and after a moment, blinked. Reid felt the hair stand up on his arms as her fixed, blind gaze cleared for a few seconds then went blank again.

"He said, 'Tell Amethyst that life often gives us second chances. She'll know what to do, and that's the clue'."

"Illuminating," Reid commented. "And do you know what to do?" He turned to Amethyst.

"Nope. As usual, he was a fount of information."

"He's not allowed to tell us anything directly," Kat informed Reid.

"Allowed?"

She shrugged. "He's also not allowed to tell us why he's not allowed to tell us anything."

"I see." He didn't, but he accepted that this was the system. He took a stab at defining the system as he saw it. "Each key has been a physical item that somehow fits into the window and works with the angle of light provided at a certain time of day during the solstice or equinox to illuminate a clue to the hiding place?"

"Yes. The first key was the big portrait of Julius in the library. The second was the locket full of lenses that led us to the architrave mechanism," Tyler passed him a binder full of the notes he had printed out, organized and even cross-referenced with colored tabs.

"Then, logically, this window should have some physical anomaly, same as the others."

Julie was amused that Reid seemed to be taking over. They had all been through this twice before, and while the search was still exciting, it was fun to watch someone going through it for the first time.

The window with its winter theme was her favorite of the four. Intricately rendered, the mostly monochromatic colors were both stark and beautiful. Bare, leafless trees in shades of black and gray speared up from the snow-covered ground into a delicately blue, wintry sky. On one branch, a brilliantly red cardinal provided an intense pop of color, which drew a viewer's eye making it the natural place for Reid to begin his scrutiny.

First, he ran his hand over the small, brightly colored bird. Nothing out of place there. Then, he carefully checked the rest of the glass panes. All normal—as were the casing and frame. Reid turned to the others and shrugged. "Now what?" He asked.

"Let Kat give it a try. She seems to have the magic touch," Gustavia suggested.

Reid stepped back as Gustavia murmured to Kat, "It's about five paces straight ahead," and Kat confidently made her way to the window.

Her fingers, sensitive from years of reading Braille, seemed to fly over the right side of the frame as she lightly touched it. Bare seconds passed before she emitted a soft, "Hmmm," and moved to the corresponding area on the left. She nodded then turned to the others, "I've found something, I think. There are two small pinholes on each side."

When Tyler stepped up, she guided his hand to the holes then stepped away so each of her friends could look.

Gustavia looked at Julie, "Paper clip or one of those hairpins Grams used to have?"

"Hairpin. I think I saw some in the library. I'll get them." Julie left the room to return quickly with several of the wide-throated, wavy, wire pins in her hand. She handed one over to Reid since he was closest to the window. His excitement was palpable as he fitted the first pin into the holes. When it fit perfectly, his eyes widened and lit up.

Gently, he pushed the pin deeper and was rewarded with a soft click.

When nothing happened, he gestured for Julie to pass him another.

He fit that one into the holes on the other side of the frame and pushed. Another click and something shifted slightly. A shove and the lower section of the right side of the frame slid away to reveal a small cavity holding something made from a thin, wrought iron rod. First Tyler gently pulled on the piece, but nothing happened, so he tried a little push. The spring-loaded bit of metal popped from the opening and spun into place. A triangular holder now sat at right angles to the window.

Something about the shape flirted with Amethyst's memory but kept sliding away before she could pin it down.

"Well, that was fun. What do you think goes here?" Reid asked.

Frowning, Julie replied, "I don't know, but it reminds me of something."

"I thought so, too," Amethyst confirmed. "Can't seem to get a visual on it, though."

"**Things just** keep getting more interesting, but I'm supposed to be leaving tomorrow," Reid looked up from inspecting the mechanism in the window frame. His eyes slid toward Amethyst, but he pulled his focus back to the room in general. "You'll keep me posted on what happens?"

A quick look passed between Julie and Tyler before Julie said, "You are welcome to stay—as long as you like—unless you already have other plans." She ignored the sharp elbow to her ribs that Amethyst delivered.

This time, when his gaze fell on Amethyst, he let it linger, intensify. "Another week, then."

It was time to come clean with her, and he dreaded that conversation.

CHAPTER EIGHT

"Amethyst, could we talk somewhere in private?"

Shrugging, she led him to the library where she curled up in one of the leather chairs, flashed him a defiant look meant to hide her true emotions, and said, "So talk."

Now that the moment was upon him, his mind went blank for a split second.

"It's about the divorce, there's something you should know." Reid would rather pull out his toenails with pliers than have this conversation, but he knew she deserved the truth. Still, there was some small hope that she might be happy to hear they were still married. Okay, maybe that was only in his wildest fantasies.

He faltered.

Amethyst impatiently waved her hand in a circular motion to indicate that he needed to get on with it. She could tell by the way he refused to meet her eye that whatever he had to say was not going to be good news.

He couldn't bring himself to say it so, instead, he told her to wait, walked out the door then returned a moment later with the papers and handed them to her.

She recognized them immediately; they still had the sticky note flags on them where he was supposed to sign. Without fully scanning the documents, she looked back at him, eyes wide and questioning.

"These are the divorce papers. I still don't know what you

are trying to say, just come to the point, please."

"I never signed them because I was still hoping you'd come back. Didn't you think it was weird when you never got a final decree in the mail?"

Amethyst sighed, "I moved twice in a short time and thought it just got lost in the mail."

Then it hit her. She was not normally this slow on the uptake, but now she understood exactly what he was trying to say.

"We're not divorced at all, are we?" She asked, surprised by the exultant surge of happiness shooting through her. The next words that popped out of her mouth were not the ones uppermost in her mind. "Well, sign them now."

Hope died with barely a sigh.

In a choked voice he asked, "Is that what you want? Are you sure?"

"Yes. No. Probably." Amethyst ran a hand through her hair. "I need a minute to think; to process this. We've been married all this time, and I had no idea." Her voice rose as shock gave way to anger.

"Is that such a bad thing?"

"You tell me." Her voice rose even higher, "I think knowing whether you're married or not is kind of a big deal. You couldn't have taken a minute out of your busy day to let me know?"

"I didn't know where you were. You disappeared without a trace. No note, no goodbye, nothing. I came home, and you were gone. It nearly killed me, Jane."

"It's Amethyst," she corrected him through clenched teeth, "And you know my parents could have reached me at any time."

"Whatever," his voice now dripped with scorn, "Call yourself whatever you want, you walked away without a second thought; just poof, you were gone. Out the door and off to start a new life with your new name."

Did he really think it had been that easy?

"Is that what you think? That on a whim, I just up and decided it was time for a new start. I was dying inside. Losing myself in some race to be Nancy Normal—Stepford Corporate Barbie Wife—dress her up and pose her but never let anyone know she is real or different or unique."

"So you just gave up."

"What do you want from me, Reid? I panicked, okay. I admit that. One day I looked in the mirror and didn't recognize my own face. I couldn't be that woman anymore. The harder I worked to become the kind of woman you needed, the more I lost myself. I figured I was doing you a favor and you'd find someone else to fit the profile."

"I didn't want someone else."

"Well, you didn't want me, either. Not the real me, anyway."

He should have known this was how she would see it and that in the simplest terms she spoke the truth.

"I see auras in the same way you need to breathe. Sure, you can hold your breath for a while but not forever. I could have lived with the clothes, the hair. Those are superficial, but you asked me to stop seeing auras. You asked me not to breathe. How can you not see the difference? You didn't want me, so I left."

"I loved you." It was his only defense.

Amethyst turned away, threw up her shields, and ruthlessly closed off the part of her that had matured over the past three years, the part of her that saw how trapped he had become. It cost a great deal of effort to paste a flat expression on her face, but she managed. It would be only too easy to give in, to run to him. Instead, she reached back inside to touch on anger; to let it build and give her the strength she needed to steel herself against him. She had determined long ago that no one would ever hurt her that way again, most especially, not Reid Grayson. Her husband.

"You mean nothing to me. I moved on a long time ago." Her tone, cool and dismissive, hid the fact that her heart was racing and her mouth was dry. She mustered every ounce of courage to keep from letting on that the sight of him brought back all the good memories along with the bad.

Moments spent laughing and planning their future, secure in the knowledge that they would always be together. Children, a house with a big backyard and a tire swing. She had intended to grow old with him, to trace the years together in the wrinkles on their faces and to look at their grandchildren and see his eyes or her mouth and be proud.

Worse, she knew he had loved her. Just not all the parts of her.

It started out innocently enough with her ability giving her insights into his office life that he found invaluable. Then had come the day she noticed the unmistakable melding of auras between two coworkers. Coworkers who were each married to other people. What people did on their own time was none of her business. The mistake had been in telling Reid about the possible affair. From then, it became, for him, like one of those magic eye posters that once seen cannot be unseen.

Eventually, the tension became so strong he felt it necessary to call both workers in for a chat. The upshot was that both resigned in humiliation leaving Reid feeling like he had been a part of something dirty.

That day was the beginning of the end. He asked her to see if she could stop seeing auras. She tried. It felt all kinds of wrong, but she found that narrowing her vision enough blocked out the special something that showed her the colors and moods of a person. He was delighted; she felt betrayed. This was a slippery slope, one she had less than zero interest in navigating.

The next day she had packed her things and run.

That she had really wanted him to come after her was something she barely admitted to herself.

Six months later, the divorce papers had gone out, and she assumed he had signed them. When the final decree never came, she just figured it had gotten lost in the shuffle during the two times she moved that year.

She had gone through all the stages of grief and now to find out it had all been for nothing was a blow.

Fists clenched and red-faced she rounded on him. All at once, the cool demeanor was gone; replaced by pure fury.

Reid's heart flared with hope. No way would she be this angry with him unless somewhere, deep down, she still cared.

So, he poked the bear; the cute little purple bear, "I only asked you if you *could* stop seeing auras; I never said you *should* stop seeing them."

"Semantics." Her eyes widened, then narrowed as she began to rant. "That's a load of crap, and you know it." As she continued to lay out his every sin, he stopped listening, the way he saw it, the more she ranted, the more she cared. It gave him hope. He could get her back.

His heart leaped again and before he could school his expression, a smile—barely more than a quirk of the lips—flashed across his face.

Amethyst saw it, and her anger ratcheted up another notch.

"You find this amusing, do you?"

Look at her, he thought, she's perfect, beautiful. My wife. For better or worse; for richer or poorer; we're still married. Whether she likes it or not.

That fire—the one that burned in her—made for a spectacular temper when she chose to unleash it, and he liked fireworks.

This time his smile was full and cheerful.

The more she ranted, the wider he smiled until she finally ran down. It was hard to stay angry with a complete fool who refused to fight back.

"What?" She asked. "Defend yourself. Don't just stand there grinning like an idiot."

What was the man thinking? Had he lost his mind?

"I love you. I've tried to stop but I can't because it has always been you. Just you—you're it for me. My wife."

His words, the truth of them shone in his aura and stopped her dead. He had never been able to lie to her, and he wasn't now. But, what was she supposed to say to him? After all this time, after not fighting for her when it counted, it was too late. Wasn't it?

Snapping her mouth shut and narrowing her eyes, Amethyst turned on her heel and walked away. Reid whistled a happy tune.

She might be mad but mad was better than indifferent. She might even think she hated him, but he was determined to win her back at any cost. All he had to offer her was love, but it would be enough. It had to be.

The man was bat-crap crazy. I tell him that I am totally over him and what does he do? Crazy man pastes on a foolish smile and refuses to accept it; she tried to stifle a smile of her own. Today he had given her a taste of the old Reid. Not corporate robot Reid who, she now realized, had come home at the end of the day wearing optimism like a thin coat of paint over a piece of weathered wood. It might hold up at a distance, but under close scrutiny, the cracks always showed. At some point, she had stopped looking; couldn't or wouldn't see that he was desperately unhappy, too. Not with her, but with his job.

Totally over him.

Those words were a big fat lie; she knew it and he knew it.

Shame washed over Amethyst at her part in their separation. Immaturity had been a factor. Had he come right out and asked her to stop seeing auras or had she overreacted? Why on earth would he want a second chance with someone who had walked away and refused to fight for their relationship?

Stuck in their endless loop, her thoughts then swung back the other way. What if he still couldn't handle her abilities? What if he asked her to stop doing the only thing that made her special again?

Amethyst shook her head to dislodge these thoughts. Ultimately, it came down to trust. Trust and forgiveness. Could there be one without the other?

If it had been anyone else calling, Tyler would have been tempted to ignore his vibrating phone; he was just as curious about what was going on in the library as everyone else, but when he saw the caller was Zack Roman, Gustavia's older brother and the cop in charge of finding Logan, he figured he'd better pick up. Estelle had already warned them about Logan's return; maybe the police had caught him.

"You want the good news or the bad news first?" Zack asked without even a hello.

"Hit me with the bad. Or wait, I bet I can guess. Logan's back in town."

"Nail on the head."

Tyler waited for the good news without telling Zack he had a source. So far, the man had not encountered either Estelle or Julius, and he was not about to be the one to have to explain to Zack that he and the others had been consorting with ghostly informants. Zack probably wouldn't believe him anyway.

"We picked up a lead and tracked him back to a rental

cottage just across the state line. Rent was paid through the end of the month, but the owner says Logan was only there for two days before he skipped out again. I'm on my way over there now. Preliminary report is that one wall was papered with photos of Julie and the rest of you. Mostly Julie and Gustavia."

Not surprising news since Julie was the mark who gotten away and Gustavia had popped on Logan's radar as a big part of the reason his con had gone south.

Zack added, "I'm counting on you and Finn to keep my sister safe, and I've ordered increased patrols for your place and hers. My gut tells me he's going to move soon and he sees her as the more vulnerable of the two. But you'd better not let Julie out of your sight."

"Goes without saying. They're all here now, I'll have a word with Finn."

"I'll keep you posted." And Zack hung up abruptly.

CHAPTER NINE

"Put some elbow grease into it." When Julius spoke into her ear the next day, Amethyst jumped violently, slammed her hip against the small table she was sanding to send it crashing over onto its side. She muttered an oath and rounded on the ghost to glare at him over crossed arms. "Didn't your mother ever teach you any manners? I thought you were gone already."

The diminutive Amethyst faced the ghost defiantly. In life, Julius had been a tall man and in spirit that had not changed. Looking at his rosy but light complexion sprinkled with the freckles that often came along with red hair, *this is a ghost* would not be the first thought to spring to mind. He appeared as solid as any living person did. He even had an aura.

"Sorry. Not quite. I needed to speak to you privately first." His apology was insincere.

"What can I do for you, Julius? Have you come to tell me you can't tell me anything as usual?" Her smile took the sting out of the words since she had seen how frustrated the inability to divulge information made him.

"No, I have a second clue for you. Where do you usually find things?" He waved a hand to dismiss the subject before continuing, "Amethyst, I need your counsel."

That got her attention as she filed the clue away.

He hesitated, and she waited patiently. Mostly.

"What is an aura?" His question was the last thing she was expecting.

Putting the explanation into a context that he might understand, she said, "I think you would most liken it to an energy field similar to the one created by an electromagnet only visible. To me, at least. It is a halo of color surrounding each person that can sometimes show me things about their emotional and physical health."

Julius nodded contemplatively then asked another surprising question, "When Estelle speaks through Kat does Kat have two auras or do they blend into one?"

Amethyst took a moment to think of the best way to describe the phenomenon.

"They overlap but only blend in the places where they are similar. Estelle's is the larger so I guess you could say it becomes superimposed over Kat's, but I can still see the distinct outline of one within the other."

"Sort of like a double exposure," he mused.

"Yes. Why?"

Ignoring her question, he asked another. "Have you ever seen anyone who wasn't like Kat but had two auras?"

"Not really. Sometimes when a couple is close to each other, their auras meld together. That looks different, though. Each aura stays with its own body but together, they mesh wherever the two people are closest, so it looks like one aura made up of two halves."

He nodded again.

"I've also seen couples, even happy couples, who have auras that won't blend at all. Oil and water. She asked again, "Why? I know there's a point to all this."

Again, he ignored the question and finally, in a quiet voice said, "They want to increase your gift."

Confused, Amethyst replied, "I don't understand."

"Nor do I, fully. They don't tell me everything."

"They?"

"Angels."

That netted him a raised eyebrow, and he muttered something about angels calling all the shots. "I'm supposed to ask your permission for them to increase your gift." Yet he appeared reluctant to do so.

Frowning at the number of questions his words prompted, and knowing from experience how little Julius was ever allowed to say, Amethyst focused on the most important one and asked, "Increase it how?"

He shrugged. "Guess that's a need to know thing, and they don't think I need to know."

Eyes flashing, she responded, "Well, I need to know. The last thing I need is some cosmic whammy. One of those in a lifetime is enough." Unaware she was doing so, Amethyst began to pluck at her own aura in an attempt to clear away the swirling fear his words had plunged her into. "I've got enough complications in my life right now without having angels adding more."

What happened next left her wide-eyed and utterly speechless. As though emerging from inside him, a new aura emanated from Julius. While Amethyst watched, it expanded and widened; a swirling rainbow of colors that slowly consumed his aura completely, then brightened until it filled her vision with blinding white.

"Ask your questions." The trumpet-like voice that commanded Amethyst seemed not to come just from Julius but from the air around him, and she would have obeyed if her mouth had not gone instantly dry and glued itself shut. As it was, all she could do was stare.

More gently this time the voice repeated, "Ask your questions. I'll answer what I can."

Now overwhelmed with the temptation to pinch herself, Amethyst resisted and did as she was told. "What do I call you?"

"I am Galmadriel." At those words, the white aura expanded once again, just enough to lightly brush against Amethyst's own. Warmth and a sense of peaceful calm washed away the fear leaving her feeling as though embraced and protected.

"You are an angel." It was a statement, not a question.

"What are you doing here?"

"My job."

"And that is…?"

"I was sent to intervene; to help those struggling against the dark." A bit more information but still less than helpful.

"What do you want from me?"

"Your help." Chagrin, faint but detectable in the angel's tone, was a surprise to Amethyst. "We would like to strengthen your gift so that you can identify and aid those battling darkness."

"How would that play out? I need specifics so I can make a proper decision."

"Your vision would expand to include more levels of the darker tones, and increase your ability to heal." Some almost undefinable nuance told Amethyst there was more; something the angel would prefer not to reveal.

"And…?"

"And we can't always predict the intensity of the changes."

"Does that mean you aren't sure what will happen?"

A moment's pause and then the angel sighed. "It is not common for us to interfere. I cannot tell you exactly how intense the experience will be; nor can I tell you the degree to which it will occur."

"Yet, you want me to just say yes," Amethyst observed with a trace of bitterness brought on by a very real fear of this new experience.

Another pause. There was more.

"And your gift would become inherent."

"Which means what, exactly?"

"Reading auras is a physical ability. If you accept the fullness of the gift, it will deepen beyond being something you can do to being something that you are. Something you will hand down through the generations."

Amethyst quirked an eyebrow as the angel continued. "You will be a Reader. Your children will also be Readers."

"It's a lot to ask." More than she could take in all at once.

"Yes," Galmadriel answered simply. "I'll leave you to decide."

"How will I contact you when I've made my choice? Through Julius?"

"Though we may meet again, there will be no need to contact me. Should you decide to accept the deepening, it will simply happen."

Uneasy about the lack of detail, Amethyst asked, "Is there anything more you can tell me about what to expect?"

"No."

"I suppose there's no grace period? Like a 30-day trial offer?"

"No, I am sorry. The choice is irrevocable." Amethyst heard a trace of humor, "so choose wisely," and with a parting command for Julius alone, Galmadriel was gone.

Shaken, Amethyst took several steps back and sank onto one of her brightly colored kitchen chairs. The entire exchange had taken only a matter of minutes, but that had been quite enough for her to handle. It wasn't every day she got the chance to talk to an angel. Wrapping her head around that experience alone was overwhelming, and now she had a big decision to make. And not quite enough information to feel comfortable making it.

She locked eyes with Julius who appeared visibly shaken by

his experience. When he had recovered enough, he finally spoke in a dry voice, "I believe I owe young Kathleen an apology. That was a most unsettling experience."

"You think?" Was the wry answer.

As the bright light surrounding him faded, Julius felt unsettled. He now had a much better idea of how Kat must have felt the day he and Estelle had first used her to make contact with Julie. He owed the brave young woman an apology and flowers or chocolate. Not that ghosts had access to the latter two.

By now, Julius knew, his energy should be flagging but the encounter with the angel, instead, left him feeling revved up, vital, almost alive again. He paced the small room, each footstep a staccato sound where normally, his presence was marked by silence.

Distracted by her own thoughts, he had made several rounds of the room before Amethyst noticed the sound. Looking up, she realized he was also muttering to himself and waving his hands around in agitation.

"What's wrong?" She asked.

"She's sending me off on an 'assignment' right when I'm needed here. Who asked her to get involved?" He paced even more furiously. "Well, okay, that would be me. But I had no idea she would send me away. Well, I'm not going. That's all there is to it. I'm needed…" He broke off as the light in the room darkened ominously.

Energy tickled up Amethyst's arms then began to build in intensity. She could feel it in the back of her throat, first a tingle then increasing pressure. She reached out to Julius, eyes widening as the sensation escalated toward pain. Julius shook his fist at nothing Amethyst could see." Fine. I'll go. Lay off."

Immediately, the oppressive energy decreased. Relieved,

Amethyst's hand rose, unconsciously, to skim her throat. She shuddered, her voice raspy and raw, "Next time you pick a fight with an angel, please do it somewhere else."

"I'm sorry." Other than an apology, he had nothing to offer. "Please tell Julie I'll be back as soon as I can. I'll have a word with Estelle before I go." His voice was gruff. "I really am sorry." Then he was gone.

For a long time, Amethyst remained immobile. Overwhelmed, she couldn't quiet her mind; her thoughts flitted back and forth between Reid's sudden appearance and the possible implications of whatever it was the angel had in mind for her.

Home. She needed it. Home and family. Not the extended family she had here with her friends. Instead, right now, she wanted her mommy.

Tomorrow was Thanksgiving.

The decision made, she quickly packed a bag, dropped Tommy off with Mishka, and made a quick phone call to Gustavia to beg off from their Thanksgiving plans. She relayed the message from Julius and without mentioning anything else, explained that she would be away for the holiday.

Feeling better than she had all week, Amethyst began the drive home.

CHAPTER TEN

Traveling these familiar roads felt like a trip back through time. The Grange Hall faded with time into a stately relic with cracked and weathered trim and paint peeling from a decade of abandonment still stood on the corner. Amethyst marked the building with a glance. It was the first of a series of touchstones that signaled she was nearing home.

A cloud of maple leaves whirled into a funnel behind her as she passed between the massive trunks lining the main street. In this town, not quite two hours north of Oakville, autumn had already passed its peak and begun to carpet the ground with golden, red, and brown crispness.

Someone had tied ribbons in the high school's blue and gold colors around every light pole and sign leading into town. Leftovers from homecoming weekend.

Turning left on Pond Road, Amethyst checked to see if anyone had painted over the misspelling on the side of the building where the seafood store used to be. No, it still read "FIHS." She rolled her eyes as she always did even while unconsciously taking comfort from the unchanging nature of her hometown.

Two miles to go. The old sawmill remained unchanged, but it looked like Mr. Farley had gotten himself a new boat. Old Pete Rawler's place still needed a roof. The shingles were curled up on the edges like the pages of a book left out in the rain.

And there it was. Home. The sprawling New England style farmhouse sparkled under a fresh coat of white paint courtesy of her two younger brothers who were still in high school. Masterminding a foul plot involving half the boys in the senior class who pranked the principal by installing his desk up on the roof of the school might have sounded like fun at the time, but it had cost them an entire summer of hard labor, scraping and painting the old house. Neither seemed the least bit repentant. The whole debacle was destined to become a town legend since they had pulled it off during school hours.

A black and white cat streaked across the yard chasing a blowing leaf.

Amethyst could have entered through the front door, but that was for company and salesmen to knock on. The family usually went in through the barn. The heavy door still stuck a bit when she pushed it open, it always did this time of year. These old farmhouses had often grown in proportion to the size of the family that lived in them. This one had a longish breezeway between the barn and the main house that smelled of hay and dust and horse.

A soft whinny called to her from the stalls where she greeted each of the occupants by name before turning toward the home and the family behind the kitchen door.

She could hear them through the door; feel their warmth reaching out from the room before she could see them. Voices raised in conversation, everyone talking and laughing at once but still managing to be heard. That's what her big, loving family was like. Only the youngest two boys still lived at home, but this was the night before the big feast when anyone who staying over for the holiday would have already arrived.

Pushing open the door, Amethyst walked into the room and into her mother's arms. For that one moment, in that one embrace, every worry fell away leaving her feeling clean and safe and quiet.

For that one moment. Then chaos erupted as the family welcomed her home. All at once.

Sally held her daughter at arm's length and scanned her face before pulling her back in for another hug. Her mother's eyes picked up on the subtle signs of tension—the tightness around her mouth and something lurking in her eyes. Her mother bear instincts kicked in. Whoever had hurt her baby had better be ready for some angry mama action.

Fall coolness outside met the moist heat of cooking inside and steamed up the windows. It smelled like heaven in the big kitchen where pots and pans full of recently harvested vegetables simmered and boiled. Farm style comfort food.

"Auntie Janey...Auntie Janey, look at my losted tooth. It got all wobbly, then it got wiggly, and then it fell right out." Niece Lexie pulled at Amethyst's pants leg until her aunt bent down to inspect the tiny bit of whiteness and bestow a hug.

In a suitably grave voice, she asked the curly headed sprite who gazed up at her with concerned brown eyes, "Are you on good terms with the tooth fairy?"

"Is she really going to sneak into my room and touch my pillow?" Lexie whispered. She seemed worried, and Amethyst had to hide a smile.

"It will all be okay. She's a very nice fairy—very gentle with pillows."

Her words comforted the child who pocketed the little tooth and scampered away.

Beneath the loud voices, there was order and organization to the meal preparation. Without appearing autocratic, Sally gently directed each activity from getting the table set to plating side dishes while she pulled a massive ham from the oven.

Before Amethyst could step forward to help, her oldest sister thrust a blanket-wrapped bundle into her arms. Her newest nephew, Emmet, blinked up from the soft folds. He was another reason for the impromptu trip. The baby was only three weeks old, and she had wanted to meet him. Oh, he smelled good; she thought as she inhaled the scent of baby and gently caressed his cheek with a fingertip. So small, so fragile, so new. She wanted one.

As she held him there, her eyes locked to his, he gave a tiny grunt, and another smell overlaid the scent she'd been enjoying.

With a big grin, she raised an eyebrow at her sister, "You knew this was going to happen, didn't you?" Her question was met with an answering grin, "Mother's instinct. She who holds him changes him. Diaper bag is over there," Allison lifted her chin to point toward a bag hanging over one of the chairs.

Cooing to the baby, Amethyst carried him to the nearest bedroom, where she gently, if inexpertly, removed all evidence of the dirty deed. When he was clean and fragrant once again, she sat there another minute, rocking him in her arms and singing a made up song of nonsense words as he nuzzled contentedly against her neck.

Envy rose up like a fog and engulfed her. Amethyst dreamed of having children of her own. Maybe not so many as the six her parents had raised, but she and Reid had decided on at least three. That dream had been pushed away with the death of her marriage. Maybe not permanently but at least for the time being.

For just the barest of moments, she allowed herself to think of what might happen if she and Reid were to work things out. A child with his eyes, her smile, and his soft, dark hair. Their babies would be beautiful.

Better to push those thoughts aside than to follow that path of heartache. No matter what the crazy man said, after not seeing each other for three years, had he expected her just to pick up where they left off? Because where they left off hadn't been anyplace good.

Still married. They were still married. Those words had been echoing in her head since falling from his lips. Every time her thoughts quieted, they boomed like a metronome.

Still married.

Still married.

It was maddening, really.

"Hey, you're holding up dinner," A voice broke into her thoughts. Her younger brother, Joe, complained, "I'm starving, come on."

"Sorry, sorry. On my way. And you're always starving. I think you'll last another minute." She sneaked in one more quiet snuggle before returning to the noise and light of the kitchen.

Sally gently tapped on her daughter's bedroom door. Forced laughter had not fooled her in the least, something was wrong, and she meant to know what it was.

"Come in." The command so soft Sally barely heard it.

She opened the door to see her daughter huddled under the covers, tears slowly coursing down her cheeks.

Two short steps carried her across the room to sit on the edge of the bed and gather the younger woman into her arms.

"Oh baby, what's happened? Tell me about it, maybe I can help."

"It's Reid."

So, the rumors were true. "I'd heard he quit his job and went off somewhere."

"*Somewhere* turned out to be Oakville. What's worse is that he somehow ended up at my friend's house. How's that for a coincidence?" Sally didn't believe in coincidence—she had that in common with Gustavia.

"That must have been quite a shock."

"You haven't heard the half of it. He never filed the divorce papers. Mom, we're still married. All this time and I had no idea."

Whatever Sally had expected, it hadn't been anything like this. Her mouth dropped open, but no words would come.

Her mother's blatant surprise actually made Amethyst feel a little better. Sometimes kindred emotions had that effect on a person.

"I just—I don't know what to say."

"I know, right? He wasn't even sorry about it."

That bit of news was no big surprise. Reid had been devastated by the split. More than once, Sally and her husband had come home to find him camped out on their front step. He had begged and pleaded with them to tell him where his wife had gone. Heartbroken and sympathetic, Sally kept her daughter's secret even though it had cost her to cause him pain when from her perspective, a bit more maturity would have solved the problem that caused them to split up in the first place. "He loved you," she said simply.

Amethyst sighed. "I know. He says he still does."

That brought no surprise as Sally simply nodded. Reid had a good heart and a father who had put him in an unenviable situation that had caused her daughter a great deal of pain. Yet, it wasn't in her heart to hate him. Not when his biggest crime had been trying to find the best way to provide for the wife he loved.

"Do you love him?"

"I don't know." That statement earned her a slanted look from her mother. "Okay, fine. I still love him. I probably always will. What if it happens again? I have to be who I am. I read auras. Can he handle what I do? I help people, and I love

81

that part of my life." She paused then said, "Mom, there's more."

Holding nothing back, she told Sally everything that had been happening in her life, from Logan and Julie's search to Gustavia and her recent family reunion. Then finally, about Galmadriel and the possibility of enhancing her aura reading ability.

Sally never batted an eye at her daughter's story of ghosts and now an angel. She had her own stories of a brush or two with the paranormal, though these were revelations for another day.

"Tell me what to do."

"Oh darling, you know I can't do that. You have to make your own decisions because you are the one who has to live with the consequences. Sometimes love is enough to see a couple through all the ups and downs of life and sometimes it isn't. If it feels right to give yourselves a second chance, then you should. Or, if you think building back the trust you once had is impossible, you need to find a way to set him free. Tonight, though, I suggest you sleep on it. See how you feel tomorrow. There's no rush to decide is there?"

"Not about Reid, he seems to think he can wait me out. Galmadriel, on the other hand, I think she will be expecting a decision soon, and I'm not sure I can give her one."

Sally countered with a question of her own, "What exactly does it mean when you clear someone's aura? How does it help them?"

Amethyst took a moment to frame her answer.

"Everyone has stress in their lives from work, relationships, health—whatever they are dealing with. Sometimes that stress goes on so long people forget how to let it go so that when the situation ends, a little bit of that stress remains. Then, each time that person encounters another stressful situation, more and more of it piles on until they become completely stuck, and it shows in their aura. I help them release that negative energy and come back to balance, to positivity. Their problems don't go away, but they have more energy to deal with them."

"Where does the negative energy go? Not into you, I hope."

With a small shudder, Amethyst answered, "No, I'd be a total wreck if I had to take on everyone's problems, but that's not how it works. When it's released, the energy becomes—I guess—inert would be the best word; not positive or negative but just neutral. It goes back to—well, it has different names—the source, God, the universe, a higher power, Mother Earth. Everyone has their own definition for it, but it all feels like the same thing to me."

"God? You stopped going to church a long time ago." It wasn't a condemnation, only an observation.

"And, I've just met an energy being who called herself an angel. What's your point, Mom?"

"No point, I'm just trying to understand."

"My problems with religion have more to do with the people involved in it than the deities. I have to believe there is some type of conscious awareness, something bigger than us."

"It doesn't seem as though an angel would offer you something that wasn't for your greater good." Sally saw it that way, and Amethyst decided not to tell her how the angel had nearly choked the life out of her with an energy burst. Maybe Galmadriel's motives were pure, but that little trick had not been very persuasive.

"I can't make the decision for you and I wouldn't even if I could. You know I'll be here for you whatever you decide. Now get some rest. You've had a rough time of it," and with a kiss on the forehead, Sally left Amethyst alone to sleep.

Even though she felt much relieved, sleep remained elusive. Maybe coming home where there were so many reminders of her life with Reid had been a bad idea. Lying on the twin bed tucked under the slanted ceiling, she counted the old-fashioned, blue roses that marched across the wallpaper in a repeating pattern. Every third rose looked like a smiling face. When she was little, she thought they looked like a line of angels watching over her. It was a comforting thought that tonight brought no solace whatsoever.

This room contained too many things that took her back in time—back to Reid. First place riding ribbons won while he stood ringside. The pink enamel frame decorated with a spiral pattern that had once held their prom picture now empty and the photograph stashed away in a breakup box on the top shelf of the closet in her tiny home.

She ran her finger over the tiny heart with an R she'd drawn on her headboard in what had turned out to be indelible ink—lightened now by repeated attempts to clean it off before her mother saw it, but still faintly legible.

The thought surfaced that their relationship was like that mark, worn by attempts to scrub it away but somehow it endured.

Melancholy was the word for this mood.

She turned off the light.

Five minutes later, she turned it back on, opened the desk drawer, and rooted around for pen and paper.

A pros and cons list. That would give her some perspective.

For the next few minutes, the only sound in the room was the tapping of her pen on the table while she stared out the window at the nearly full moon. At last, she scratched out a single entry on each list.

Pros: He loves me

Cons: He loves me

Crumpling the paper into the smallest, tightest possible ball and lobbing it into the trash did not provide the hoped-for stress release. Meditation finally brought sleep but not for a long time.

It was a cloudless autumn Sunday. A robin's egg blue sky played backdrop against torch-shaped trees, some still clothed in saturated reds and yellows. Rolling hills to the right of the two-lane country road arched softly against the blue, while wheat-colored fields bordered on the left. Unseasonable weather kept it warm enough for open-windowed driving, the air hung with the dry, powdery smell rising from the crisp fallen leaves that blanketed parts of the road. It was the kind of day that made a person thankful to be alive.

Too preoccupied with her thoughts, Amethyst barely noticed.

Instead, various scenarios played themselves out in her imagination. Reid would win her back by promising his undying love, and they would have three beautiful children. Two boys and a girl; all with the ability to see auras.

Or, they wouldn', and she would die a lonely, childless, cat lady.

That's just ridiculous, it's not like he's the only man in the world, Amethyst chided herself for nihilistic thinking and ignored the small voice in the back of her mind that insisted on suggesting that for her, he just might be.

To take her mind off the constant seesaw of emotions, she stopped at her favorite flea market. Seven or eight small sheds ringed a semi-circular parking area. Ranged around the sheds, more vendors had set up canopy tents stuffed with tables and racks of items from the sublime to the ridiculous. One vendor had a sizable collection of Fiesta ware and an even larger collection of bottles containing medical specimens. Where else could you buy a surgically removed appendix for the small sum of $25.00 and why was she tempted to buy one?

An hour slipped by as she pored through the multitude of offerings. The vendor at the next to last shed in line had a handful of cat related items. Tommy was about to become the proud owner of a carpet-covered kitty tree. He'd probably hate it. Or, more accurately, he'd turn his back on it with an expressive flick of the tail, give her that look, the one that clearly said, "Human, please," and then as soon as she wasn't looking, climb all over it.

With a smile and some shameless flirting, she talked the guy down to ten bucks and got him to help load it in her car where it stuck out the back window a bit.

It may have been the heavenly smells coming from the food truck at the far end of the market or just that she had lost track of time and it was well past lunch that made her stomach lurch and growl.

Picking her way past several interesting looking vendors and refusing to get distracted again, Amethyst approached the source of those amazing smells to order a gourmet mushroom burger with sweet potato fries.

The food, shopping, and fresh air helped clear her mind. If she cut away all the noise, what remained was truth. She was married, and Reid wanted to stay that way. Problem was, he still felt like cheesecake to her—something she might crave but would probably be better off without.

No, that wasn't fair.

Sitting alone at a picnic table in the middle of a glorified yard sale was not the place one might expect to have an epiphany but the anonymity of this place—busy but with her as an island at its edge—allowed her to look back and evaluate the past objectively. He hadn't meant to hurt her. The hot redness of shame crept along her neck. She had run away like a child and abandoned her husband, yet he still wanted her back.

Knowing that he did made her heart soar. For a minute. Until she realized just how much distance there was between the two of them. Before she could talk herself out of it, she texted Julie and asked for Reid's number, keyed it into her phone, quickly composed another text:

We need to talk. Dinner tonight? —Amethyst

His response was swift in coming:

Sure. 6pm?

Amethyst replied:

I'll meet you at Julie's place.

A flock of butterflies launched themselves into frantic flight in her stomach. Wait—flock? Was that the right term? Herd? No, maybe a flight. To try and settle the fluttering, she looked it up on her phone. The technical term was kaleidoscope. Pretty word that sounded exactly right.

The tickling lurch of nerves added a level of excitement to combat the dread she was feeling. If she could just concentrate on the good memories—and there were plenty of those—instead of the painful ones, this dinner would go well. If—such a little word with big meaning.

When she picked up Tommy from Mishka, he treated her to his patented, how-dare-you-leave-me stare then refused to look at her again. Leaving him to get acquainted with his new toys, Amethyst tore into her closet to choose some proper date attire. Bits of purple clothing flew onto the bed, missed the bed, landed on the floor and by the time she was done, one pair of leggings was dangling from a lamp.

To add another complication, Tommy leaped onto the pile, rolled and came back up onto his feet in a playful mood. He was impossible to resist, so she moved the clothes and took time for a game of kitty toy toss before deciding on a pair of leggings in vibrant, electric purple. These she topped with a long, embroidered tunic with a Nehru collar.

By the time she pulled to a stop in front of Hayward House,

the butterflies had turned into pterodactyls—big, vicious beasts with claws and teeth and beaks. Whatever the group name for those might be, she knew it could not be as pretty sounding as a kaleidoscope.

A date. It had been a very long time since the prospect of going out to dinner had caused such a nervous reaction.

The drive to Hayward House passed way too quickly.

Julie answered the door, provided a supportive hug and led Amethyst to the living room where Reid was waiting. Her whispered comment of, "He's nervous, too," did help release some of the tension but the sight of him ratcheted it right back up to the level of a scream, and she actively had to resist the temptation to go to him and run a hand through his carefully groomed hair.

Reid swallowed twice and admitted to himself that purple had just become his new favorite color.

"Let's take my car," he suggested as he followed her out the door. The day remained warm enough for top-down driving and being male, he wanted to show off his wheels.

"Sure, if you let me drive," she waggled her eyebrows at him, and he remembered her affinity for fast cars. Glancing over at the battered Honda, he knew she hadn't had the means to indulge herself recently, so he tossed her the keys.

"Mmm," Amethyst couldn't hold back a hum of appreciation for the finely tuned machine as she downshifted and stomped the pedal. The car leaped under her control as, head back and laughing, she poured on the speed. "Oh, you're a pretty baby, aren't you?" She crooned to the car, nearly forgetting the man who watched her with an indulgent grin lighting up his face.

The wind teased strands of hair across her face, and she shook them off with a head toss. The drive into Oakville was all too short; she had barely enough time to explore the car's capabilities before pulling into the municipal parking lot.

"Fun ride." It was a compliment, and he took it as one. "I'm thinking Italian or seafood. Any preference?"

What he wanted was some privacy.

"Someplace quiet." Not Tassone's, then. Great Italian food with a family atmosphere made it a busy venue.

"Seafood it is." She led him a short way down the street toward a door decorated with fishing nets and floats. From the front, the place looked like a hole in the wall, but once inside, he could see the restaurant opened up. The entire, bow-shaped back wall was a series of floor to ceiling windows providing a panoramic view of the lake where several local sailboat owners were taking advantage of what might be the last warm weekend before cocooning their toys for the winter. Another hour or so before sunset saw the light wind gently tugging at sails, belling them while the boats skimmed over the lake's slightly choppy surface. Framed by brilliant autumn foliage, colorful triangles cheerfully contrasted with the slowly deepening blue of the sky; each moment presented a new, soothing image.

Efficient staff seated them at a table with an unobstructed view, and the couple settled in to watch the bustling activity as boaters maneuvered their way in to tie off at the piers.

Amethyst tried to relax. It seemed imperative she calm her jangling nerves enough to say what needed to be said.

"Reid, I…" She broke off as plates of succulent seafood were placed in front of them and by the time the waiter walked away, she felt as though the moment had passed. Without thinking, they fell into an old habit; she ordered one dish and he another. When the food came, they each scraped half their choices onto the other's plate.

For the next few minutes, all conversation centered on the food. Reid wanted to remind her of some of her more spectacular cooking failures, but he wasn't sure she was ready for a walk down memory lane. He was right.

Once the small talk was exhausted, Amethyst started to feel squirmy. Words needed to be said. Apologies and explanations to be made. So, why was her head completely empty?

A furtive movement outside the window drew her attention. It couldn't be. She looked again.

Logan. It looked like Logan stumbling past the glass. With a choked cry, she threw her napkin on the table and bolted out the door leaving Reid just sitting there with his mouth hanging open.

Had he said something wrong? He didn't think so.

Reid tossed a handful of bills on the table and followed her out the door. If she thought she could just walk away from him again, she was in for a surprise.

CHAPTER ELEVEN

The restaurant door slammed shut behind him making a loud cracking sound that he ignored. Which way had she gone? He glanced left but turned right to stalk down the sidewalk, anger lending volume to the beat of his shoes on the pavement.

Ten long paces, then twenty before he saw furtive movement ahead. Good grief, the woman stood out. What on earth was she doing? It wasn't as if he planned on forcing himself on her. They had been enjoying a very nice meal and some light conversation and getting to know each other again until she freaked out for whatever reason.

"Amethyst…" He called out.

She turned and motioned for him to be quiet. It was then that he realized this might not be about him at all.

When he reached her, she pointed and whispered, "Logan."

"What? Are you sure?" Every ounce of anger drained away. She must have seen Logan pass by the window at the restaurant.

"It's him. Go. Call Tyler, have him call Zack."

"Are you crazy? I'm not leaving you here alone."

"Just go. We can't pass up this chance. Walk down the street, just far enough so he won't hear you."

Dismissing Reid with a wave of her arm and making it clear she expected him to do what she'd asked, Amethyst turned back to watch the other man.

Well, she could order him around if she wanted to, but if she thought he was going to leave her there alone, she had better think again. Not happening, not for a single minute.

Stepping into the shadow of a doorway, he pulled out his phone. No service.

Not for half a block farther down and that was as far he dared to go. Any farther and he wouldn't be able to keep an eye on her.

Reid turned back to look toward where Amethyst had been standing, but she wasn't there. He had only looked away long enough to pull up Tyler's name on his contact list. She couldn't have gone far. His heartbeat sped up at the thought of his wife taking on a dangerous criminal.

Tyler picked up on the second ring, and Reid only took the time to bark out, "Logan is on the street near the wharves right now," and hung up.

Then, he hurried back to where he had last seen her.

Once Reid walked away to make the call, Amethyst turned back to watch Logan advance slowly down the street, his movements furtive. If he knew she was trailing him, he never let on. Twice, when he inadvertently stepped into a pool of light, she could see his lips moving. Was he talking to himself?

After a moment, she became aware of a humming noise that seemed to come from everywhere and nowhere at once. Logan heard it, too. She could tell by the way turned his head from side to side as though looking for something.

When she tried to describe it later, she said it sounded like a thousand bees were flying overhead.

The buzzing got louder, closer. Instinctively, she ducked. Nothing was there, but something surely was coming right at her. The air rippled as a wave of energy rushed forward, then stopped to hover a hair's breadth away. Galmadriel's voice, like the gong of a bell, sounded in her head.

"Do you accept?"

This was it. Her moment of truth.

Amethyst closed her eyes. The powerful wave of energy seethed and writhed in front of her as though it was waiting for something—and none too patiently.

Saying yes meant changing her life in ways that the angel could not or would not explain. It was a gamble, though the idea of helping more people appealed to her sense of community. Using her ability to help others felt right and made up for a lot of the teenage angst that had left her feeling like an outcast.

Softer now, "Do you accept?"

Was she ready to take control of her life, her gift, and all the messiness that might come with it?

The pressure built another notch, but she sensed that if her answer was no, she would not be harmed.

Galmadriel asked for the final time, "Do you accept?"

"Yes." She whispered and lifted her face just the slightest bit, just enough to touch it to the mass of energy.

For an instant, the buzzing returned as the shifting mass swelled then slammed into her with what felt like tornado force. For less than a second or several lifetimes, she wasn't sure which, it whirled around her before bonding itself to her every molecule and filling her with light.

Even with her eyes still tightly closed, she saw stars against her lids as the brilliance flared and blinded. Then, leaving the tang of ozone in the air, it was over.

The enormity of what she had just done slammed into her. She had accepted the deepening of her gift. There would be no hiding it now, no turning it off the suit the sensibilities of any man.

She opened her eyes and at first, saw absolutely nothing. Still dazzled by the light, they had trouble focusing. Then with each blink, the effect subsided, and she began to see what the angel had given her

Every living thing glowed with aural rainbows of color. Grass, trees, even rocks gave off some halo.

There were so many so close together that they almost melded into a single, amorphous whole.

Something tingled at her senses, and she turned to see Reid standing nearby. Her focus fell on his aura.

Such beauty and warmth. More than she could have ever imagined. Then she glanced toward where she had last seen Logan and the beauty rapidly faded as the chill of evil washed over her.

Dread tingled into a wave that rippled across her body leaving goose bumps in its wake. The sensation bordered on painful.

Unprepared, she had no shield against the frigid darkness, and it engulfed her, threatened to force itself into her before she could look away.

Flung almost to the edge of consciousness, an eternity passed before the spark within her flexed then flared into an inferno of light.

Reid watched it all happen; he saw the energy as it rippled the air, faintly heard the buzzing and now he could see and feel the light as though it was a living, breathing thing inside her. If this was what an aura looked like, he envied her ability to see them.

As the light inside and around her expanded, he felt privileged to experience her transformation and if she thought he couldn't handle it or her auras, she was delusional. She was everything.

Needing to go to her, he tried to take a step forward only to discover that he could not lift his foot. A barrier, an invisible wall had shot up between them, and he was powerless to move.

Rooted and helpless to act, he could do nothing but stand and wait. When she opened her eyes, he felt the hair prickle on the back of his neck. Echoing light flared eerily in her eyes before she blinked slowly and they returned to normal, then fell on him like a thunderclap. In that moment, he realized Amethyst had put up the wall. Maybe unintentionally, but it had been her doing.

Enigmatically, she smiled at him and turned away to search the darkness where Logan had been only moments before. As she did, the barrier began to fade.

With a wrench, Reid finally managed to take a hesitant step and then another. Each movement forward an effort that finally ended long moments later with him reaching her only to find she stood rigidly; her eyes fixed on the point where Logan had faded into the shadows.

Logan was there, she could feel him, or more correctly, she could feel what was inside of him. Even through the thick darkness it generated, if she concentrated, she could see him.

All the warmth drained out of her to be replaced by bone-chilling cold.

Intuition told her the invading presence had sensed her ability to see it.

That lurking, leering, smear of hatred was now directed at her. A stronger chill shot through her already shivering limbs as Reid wrapped his arms around her offering the only thing he had available, the heat from his body.

It helped but not enough. Not nearly enough.

Darkness dragged her down, emptied her out, and left her even colder than before.

There, a glimmer of color flashed as the wash of light from a passing car shone off his skin and this time, she saw the auras.

Little more than a pallid shadow of color fought against the thing that held him, its aura blacker than night.

Amethyst was rooted to the spot, unable to tear her eyes away. A bell sounded in her head as the auras pulled back to show her more—a nightmare image, Logan and the thing inside him.

The lowering dusk faded against the light of her new, angel-given vision.

The scene imprinted itself on her brain.

Logan, mouth open and screaming, his face a mask of terror as he struggled against a figure dressed in filthy rags. It was the spirit of a man, not a demon.

She blinked, and it was as though a filter fell over her eyes that allowed her to see the spirit's aura, not only as it was now, but as a living history of a life. From the bright spark of infancy to the broad colors of manhood. Layer upon layer, each experience, the good and the bad defined by color and texture as each built upon the one before until some event brought a touch of the black. His past scrolled before her eyes. The man had not turned from the darkness, choosing instead to embrace it, to bind his own fate to evil.

Then, Logan's auric history played itself out like a movie stuck on fast forward. She watched him flirt with shades of gray but never black. Not until it was forced on him.

Julius had been right. Logan may not deserve it, but they needed to help him.

Amethyst blinked again, and the auras receded until she only saw the two men. Separate now; standing side by side.

Logan was gaunt, his body whittled away under loosely hanging clothing. His once well-groomed hair, now lank and greasy, fell nearly to the collar of his shirt. Beside him, the ghost wore a cape over simple breeches tucked into a pair of worn boots. A sword hung at his side, but he did not seem to need it as he held the struggling Logan firmly in his control.

Turning his head, the spirit's eyes locked with Amethyst's, the hatred in them boring a hole through her. His face was as dirty as his clothing; the straggly beard affixed to his chin as matted as his hair. Eyes dark and shining like the carapace of a beetle held a fierce intelligence and cunning under a pair of bushy dark brows but also carried surprise. She could see him. How was she able to do that? She read that thought as if he had created it in words of white written on the blackness.

The brief moment was over as the car passed, pulling the light away from the dark corner. Amethyst felt them turn to walk away into the night. Galmadriel had given her the ability to heal the blackness but not the knowledge of how. Yet, she had to try. Out of sheer instinct, she threw her light into the darkness where, for one brief moment, it filled the void. Logan's eyes pleaded with her to finish it, to free him completely before her energy depleted and if she had known how she would have done it. Instead, she lost the ability to focus.

Her knees buckled but Reid caught her before she fell. He reveled in the chance to hold her close. Her skin felt like ice, so he yanked off the light jacket he was wearing, wished he had something heavier and wrapped it around her while gathering her in. The need to warm her, to quell her violent shivering, was strong within him.

Always scornful of how characters in action movies seemed to find the time for a sexual encounter during the thick of things, he now understood how heightened emotions and a desire to protect could easily turn to a desire for other things.

Filing the urge under the heading of *this is not the time for that,* he carried her to the car and after some awkward maneuvering, managed to get them both into the passenger seat with her still in his arms.

Heat, she needed heat. Okay, he thought, start the car. He squirmed in the cramped quarters and confined space until he could get a hand in his pocket and pull out the keys. Reid stabbed at the ignition switch with the key and missed by a mile. He made a vow to practice becoming ambidextrous; you never knew when you might need to do something left-handed.

Finally, after several tries, he managed to coax the engine to life and fire up the heater, all the time murmuring words of comfort into Amethyst's ear. Was it his imagination or were the shudders beginning to subside?

Gently, he cupped her face in his hand, willing his warmth into her as she began to pull herself back to the present. Enough light fell from the street lamps illuminating the parking lot that he could see her eyes flutter then open.

She whispered, "Cold. So cold," as she burrowed deeper into his body.

"Shh, baby. Just hang on," He encouraged as he tried not to think about the intimate contact of their bodies. She clung, so tightly he could feel the hammering of her heart.

The night was still warm enough that if it hadn't been for the chill coming off her body, he thought he might have melted into a puddle.

Time stretched out into long minutes before enough warmth seeped into her cold-tightened body that she was able to relax into her breath. She inhaled deeply then, without thinking, relaxed even more as the unique scent of him washed over her.

A hint of soap, a dash of shampoo—something with a faint odor of lime—and the indefinable essence that was just him and home and life itself. Forgetting everything but that feeling, she nuzzled his neck until his breath hitched and his hand slid under the jacket to stroke down her back.

All it would have taken was one small movement to bring their lips together, and he didn't want to resist the temptation, but this probably wasn't the time even if she was only a whisper away.

In the end, he didn't have to resist because she was the one who gave in to the need and moved that fraction of distance to lay her lips on his.

Once the kiss started, he couldn't help but take it deeper, and she went there willingly with him, mingled her breath with his, listened to the sound of their thundering hearts in the small space.

Reid knew he had to stop or he never would so he eased back, just a bit, then a bit more.

Tenderly, he brushed the hair back from her face, gently turning it to gaze into her eyes. "Better?" She nodded, biting her lip as she pulled her awareness back from him to ponder what she had seen.

CHAPTER TWELVE

Silence lay over the pair of them like a thick blanket during the car ride back to Hayward House. All the way there, Amethyst worried about how to control the intensity of her new level of aura vision. It had not come with an instruction manual. Everything looked incredibly beautiful, but even beauty can be overwhelming when it is everywhere at once. She had to concentrate because the motion of the car against all that color was making her sick. Squeezing her eyes shut and pressing her hands over them helped reduce the nausea but not enough.

Reid noticed. "Do you need me to stop?" He slowed down until she began to look a little less green. Was he callous if part of his concern was that she not chuck her seafood in his car?

About halfway back to Hayward House, she realized there was no way she would be driving home by herself. Not if she couldn't even open her eyes.

"Pull over. Please." Amethyst stumbled from the car and into the cooling night air. The crisp chill felt invigorating. Even in velvety, moonlight-free darkness, the colors were overwhelming. Instead of getting used to them, she thought they were becoming more intense, making it harder to focus.

Dizziness made her stagger and lose her balance. She would have gone down if a strong pair of hands hadn't caught her. She thought it was Reid supporting her, but when she managed to pry her eyes open just the slightest bit, she saw him standing by the car, mouth open and staring. Odd, she thought, wasn't it dark out a minute ago?

Now, it was as though a spotlight shone all around her and she moaned as the brilliance lit up even more shifting bands of color.

Amethyst gagged and dragged her eyes toward the source of that light, then upward until they latched on to the face of the one who held her. Galmadriel gazed down at her with an unreadable expression. The angel settled the woman on her feet with gentle concern then spoke as gently as she could.

"Speak your concern."

Stammering, Amethyst said, "I can't unsee or even mute the auras at all. I can only see layer after layer after layer of color that shifts and shifts. This upgrade is making me sick from the constant movement—I can't focus on anything. I'm too disoriented."

"There's little enough I can do for you, but I will try my best." Galmadriel laid both hands on Amethyst's head for a moment then drew them away slightly leaving a trail of light to show the path they had taken.

Within moments, the excess of color and motion stabilized. Heaving a great sigh of relief, Amethyst said, "Thank you. Will it always be like this? Or will I gain more control over time? Having the entire world look like a moving rainbow barfed on it will get old in a hurry." Her attempt at humor amused Reid who tried to smile with a face that wouldn't quite respond properly but failed to elicit any change of expression whatsoever from the angel who gazed back at her, head tilted to one side considering.

Determined to keep her composure under scrutiny, Amethyst lifted her chin slightly but otherwise remained still. She felt as though the angel was measuring her but refused to wilt under the pressure.

Finally, Galmadriel pronounced, "I have placed a temporary block on your energy centers. It will not hold forever and will reduce your new ability to a level slightly above the original. Accepting the upgrade, as you call it, is only the first step. You must now embrace what you have become in order to control your vision. I cannot help you with that."

Turning this new information over in her mind, Amethyst asked another question, "If I have not done so when the block is gone, will the layers and motion become permanent?"

Galmadriel refused to answer directly, "Embrace your gift. Make use of the reprieve you have been granted but do not fail to act promptly. Much depends upon you."

"Anyone ever tells you that ambiguity is not a virtue?" She wanted answers, not vague portents. Frustration colored her tone with a bit of snark before she remembered stories of angels smiting bad guys. Better shut up before she got—smited? Or was it smote? Well, whichever, she didn't care to find out firsthand.

A hint of a smile slid across the angel's face before she schooled her features. Maybe she did have a personality, Amethyst thought, or she can read minds.

"There will be three tests to prove that you have embraced your gift and you will know when you have passed each one."

"Will I be visited by the ghost of Christmas past?" Sarcasm dripped from Amethyst's tongue. Let the smiting commence.

Now Galmadriel smiled broadly. Yes, there was definitely a sense of humor there. "You have already been visited by two ghosts and an angel. Is that not enough for you? Maybe I should send a unicorn."

That sparked an answering grin, "Are there unicorns? My friend Gustavia would…" she paused and thought better of it before crudely mentioning uncontrollable bodily functions to an angel "…love to see one." Dodged a bullet there.

"I can neither confirm nor deny, so your friend's pants are probably safe for the time being." Now Amethyst was certain she saw a twinkle in the angel's eye and that she could read minds.

The angel probably had places to be, but Amethyst still had to ask, "I saw a man inside Logan—you know who that is?" There was an answering nod. "I could see two auras and then two men struggling inside him. It was quite clear. I think Logan is possessed. Maybe by a demon." Her voice rose to make it a question though she was sure it had not been a demon.

"Not a demon. An Earthwalker."

"A what, now?"

"Earthwalker. It is what we call a spirit who deliberately turns from the light."

"Okay. So, what do we do about the Earthwalker?"

"Pass the three tests, and we shall see." And, with a sober smile and a flash of light, Galmadriel was gone.

From somewhere behind her, Amethyst heard Reid's low whistle. She'd totally forgotten about him. She turned and as the last of the angel's light faded, noted that he looked about as shaky as she had felt earlier. No longer dizzy and overwhelmed she found his wide-eyed shock slightly amusing especially knowing it probably mirrored her own at that first meeting with Galmadriel.

"You keep interesting company these days."

Her voice coming out of the darkness was solid, dry. "Just another Sunday." A pause. "Still want to make it work? With all the craziness and complications? No one would blame you if you turned and ran."

Reid opened the car door to let the interior light spill out. He needed to see her face. What he saw was her best blank expression. He knew it well, it was the one she used when she was trying to cover up pain or anger or fear.

He shrugged then looked down at his feet. "These aren't my running shoes, guess I'll stick around."

"Your choice. Let's get moving before anything else happens." Amethyst swung back into the car and shut the door firmly.

This whole increasing her level of abilities thing was only more complicated by dealing with her ex—no wait—her current husband. Necking in the car like teenagers was the cherry on top of that particular sundae. Still, cherries made tasty treats and so did Reid, come to that.

Minutes later, they pulled back into the drive at Hayward House. Gustavia's "baby" was quite deliberately parked behind Amethyst's car. No chance of slinking home to adapt and adjust in private. Reid rolled to a stop, switched the ignition off, and asked the one question she was not ready to deal with. "Where do we go from here?"

About five different answers, each one more sarcastic than the last, wanted to pop out of her mouth as her stomach fluttered with nerves, but she resisted the urge and gave him the honest one. "I need some time to adjust to everything that's going on."

His jaw clenched; she saw it and reassured him. "Not distance, just time. Can we just let things happen naturally? Without expectations?"

Her words soothed some of the tension inside him. They still had a conversation ahead of them—probably more than one—before any real resolution could happen, but if the door was still open, he could wait.

"**...and so now** I just have to pass the three tests, whatever they are." Listening to the words hang in the air for a moment, Amethyst realized exactly how ridiculous her story sounded when she said it out loud.

"When this is all done, I fully expect Gustavia to write a book about it." Her flippant attitude did not fool her friends. Pale skin and trembling hands were dead giveaways to her state of mind.

"Did Zack find anything? With everything that had happened, it would have raised more questions than it answered if I had stayed to wait for him."

"No, he was long gone before the police arrived."

After a cup of tea and some time in a safe space, she felt calm enough to drive home. All she wanted to do was climb into bed, listen to Tommy purring, and sleep for at least a week.

The first chance he had to get Tyler alone, Reid cornered the man. "Just how dangerous is this Logan character?"

"He tried to break in here but he didn't know about Lola, and she got the jump on him," Tyler told him about Gustavia's booby trap.

"Then he cut Gustavia's brake lines. She and Kat—well, it was a near thing. If Gustavia hadn't had defensive driving training, they might have been killed. After that, he bashed up her car with a baseball bat. We put in an alarm system here, and Gustavia's got one as well."

A chill of dread settled in Reid's belly as he asked the next question, "Does he have it in for Amethyst, too?"

"Not so far. I think he blames Gustavia for turning Julie against him and sees her as a threat, but at the same time, he thinks she is the more vulnerable of the two. Funny, he doesn't appear to have the stones to come after me. I wish he would."

His words went a long way toward settling Reid's nerves. "I'd like to stick around a bit longer. See what I can do to help. If you don't think Julie would mind."

Tyler knew exactly what motivated this decision. A woman he wanted to protect and the irresistible call of a treasure hunt. It hadn't been so long since he'd been drawn in by them. Still was if he was being honest.

"Consider yourself invited."

"And you'll square it with Julie?"

"No worries." Tyler wondered what Amethyst would think about this new turn of events. He could tell something had happened between the two of them, but neither one was talking.

CHAPTER THIRTEEN

During the ride into the city, Amethyst fingered the ten-dollar bill in her pocket knowing it was evidence that she lacked any sort of impulse control. When had Kat proposed a bet that Julie would find a wedding gown that fit her perfectly right off the rack it seemed too good to pass up. There was no way. Wedding gowns always required a little something to fit perfectly and not to say that Julie's figure wasn't well proportioned—it was—but that's not how these things worked. A safe bet if ever there was one.

For their first stop, they were going to be meeting Gustavia's great aunt and the cousin, Beth, who owned that cute little boutique. Beth had agreed to hook them up with a friend who owned, in her opinion, the best bridal shop.

Still slightly nervous around her new extended family, Gustavia was nevertheless excited to introduce them to her friends. Valerie, who by all accounts, was the complete opposite of her twin, the infamous grandmother who had raised Gustavia in a palatial but cheerless home, greeted them warmly.

The bridal shop Beth guided them to was only two doors down from her own business, and from the front, it didn't look like much. The tiny showroom was clean enough and well decorated, but with only three gowns on display, Amethyst knew that if this was the only place they shopped, her ten dollars was about to be doubled.

Beth led them through the showroom and made for the back of the store calling out as she went, "Hey Luce, we're here." From somewhere distant, they heard a muffled voice, "I'm in the back," and followed the sound.

Beyond a small but spotlessly clean changing area, was another doorway and the second they stepped through it, Amethyst felt the uncanny sensation of her hair lifting off her head to stand on end, then just as quickly, it plastered itself to her scalp. Looking around the huge room bursting with row after row of gowns encased in protective bags, she knew it was the static from all that plastic that affected her finely textured hair.

Great, now I've got helmet hair or worse, she thought.

The huge space extended behind the storefronts on either side to create a vast warehouse of dresses. The ten-dollar bill in her pocket suddenly felt less secure.

"This is my friend, Lucy. She'll take excellent care of you. Trust her, she always finds her customers the perfect dress. They call her the bride whisperer. You'll stop by my place again before you leave?" This last was directed at Gustavia who nodded but her attention was on the bounty around her and Amethyst could see her weighing whether or not it would be rude to try on a few dresses herself.

Lucy was a tall, extraordinarily thin woman whose mannerisms were vaguely birdlike. Without even a "hello," she cocked her head appraisingly at the group then turned directly to Julie and asked the date of the wedding.

"Two days after Christmas. I know that doesn't leave much time," Julie apologized.

Lucy shrugged off the time constraints as she motioned for Julie to do a slow turn. Lucy appraised the bride-to-be then nodded. "Make yourselves at home; I'll go pull some options." She waved a hand around the room pointing out different areas with designer names on the walls. "Browse around, have some champagne, try on anything you like."

"Was it just me or was that weird? She didn't even ask which one of us was the bride." Julie whispered loudly, eyes round with surprise.

Gustavia grabbed Kat and peeled off toward the Vera Wang section while Amethyst followed Julie toward a much larger changing area than the one they had just passed through. Overwhelmed by the number of selections, Julie stopped then turned in place with no idea where to start.

Determined to make the most of her time, Gustavia set a land speed record choosing several gowns for Julie to try on then succumbed to the urge and picked out one for herself. Just in case.

Since Julie was still leafing through racks, Amethyst took the dresses from Gustavia and sorted through them.

"No, this one is out. It has big puffy sleeves, the skirt is too full, and there's too much bling." The dress just screamed princess and Amethyst knew Julie didn't see herself as the Cinderella type.

"What about this one, it's elegant," Gustavia insisted as she held out a straight column with a striking neckline that looked amazing on the hanger.

"Fine." Amethyst hung the dress in the changing area then dragged Julie over to try it on, but with the stiff neckline standing up behind her head, she looked like she had gone from princess to evil queen.

Lucy was still roaming around somewhere deep in the warehouse area when Estelle shimmered into view next to Kat. She glanced around to make sure no one else would see her and said, "Kathleen, I'm sorry I didn't get here sooner. Are you ready?"

Having channeled Estelle multiple times now, Kat opened up

to let the spirit slide into her consciousness and with tears in their eyes, Kat and Estelle hugged Julie then hit the racks to become part of the gown choosing process.

Five dresses later, Julie had ruled out anything with an exaggerated train, bustle, or that was too slim-fitted to walk in easily. The last thing she wanted to do was spend the evening dragging her dress along behind her. Exaggerating her backside by affixing a large lump of fabric to it held even less appeal, and there was no way she intended to mince down the aisle in anything so tight she couldn't take a full step.

Lucy had already pulled a dress—the dress, in fact—but held back awhile before presenting her choice to give the group more time to enjoy themselves. They were lovely women who laughed easily and with great affection.

After trying on seven or eight dresses, Julie was getting overwhelmed, and that was when Gustavia grabbed her own choice and sneaked into the dressing room. When she came out looking like the doll on top of a bohemian wedding cake, Amethyst gave in and selected something for herself.

Now with the three of them wearing white, they turned on Kat.

"Oh, no. You three are crazy. Leave me out of this. You know I'm never getting married."

Amethyst snorted, now that was a bet she could win. Kat was not destined to be alone.

"Let's put this to a vote. Everyone in favor of Kat trying on a dress?" Amethyst intoned.

Three hands lifted in the air. Then, to her chagrin, Estelle lifted her own hand as well.

"It seems you have been outvoted." Amethyst leafed through a few racks and picked out a beautiful sweep of white with a beaded bodice. "Go forth and dress yourself." She gently pushed Kat into the dressing room.

When Lucy swept in pulling a wheeled rack hung with a single opaque, zippered bag behind her, she found all four women dressed in white and posed like Charlie's Angels in front of the mirror.

To their credit, they looked slightly embarrassed to be caught playing. "I think I have just the thing, follow me." A grinning Lucy scooped up the bagged dress and led Julie into the fitting room.

Once changed back into her own clothes, Amethyst slumped down on a white chaise and sipped at her glass of champagne. All this wedding dress shopping made her slightly wistful. Eloping had robbed her of this experience.

"At least with Julie, you know she won't make us wear one of those ugly bridesmaid dresses. She's not vain enough for that." It was a simple truth, but Amethyst raised her voice enough to let Julie hear the comment. With three older siblings, her closet already contained a couple of clunkers.

After a few minutes, Julie reappeared in the dressing room doorway looking radiant in a fall of sparkling, icy white.

The dress was perfect in every way. A very simple, long-sleeved top in soft, stretchy material with a gently rounded neckline rose above a graceful bell-shaped skirt that was just slightly longer in the back. The only embellishments were a row of buttons down the backs of the sleeves and a narrow sash at the waistline with a small bow in the back. It was simple and plain, but those qualities were what made it elegant.

"Oh, Julie. It's spectacular." Amethyst teared up a little.

Estelle took over Kat's body for just a moment and, stepping forward, pulled Julie into a fierce hug. Amethyst heard her whisper, "My darling girl," and that was all it took to have the tears spilling over. It must have hit Gustavia the same way because, despite her beaming smile, tears were streaming down her face as well.

Even Lucy looked a little misty.

Once the hugging ended, Lucy asked Julie to stand on a low pedestal while she assessed the dress to see how much tailoring might be needed. After circling several times, she lifted up the hem a little to inspect Julie's shoes. "You'll be wearing these same heels?"

Julie nodded.

Lucy circled again. She stood behind Julie and smoothed her hands across the shoulders. She tugged the waistline gently and twitched the folds of the skirt.

"Then this is a first because I can't find a thing that needs adjusting."

Rolling her eyes, Amethyst pulled the ten from her pocket and handed it over to Kat who accepted the money with a self-satisfied smile.

"No need to gloat."

Julie went back into the dressing room to remove the dress then it was her turn to recline on the chaise and watch while the others tried on bridesmaid dresses. Red and silver were her wedding colors, but she had not considered just how many shades and textures there were of each.

Gustavia, of course, gravitated toward bright, scarlet reds. Kat picked out muted silvery grays, and Amethyst found a rack of red dresses with white fur trim that were a bit too on the nose for a Christmas wedding.

"There's an art," Lucy explained to Julie as they watched Gustavia pawing through the racks, "to choosing the dresses your attendants will wear. I can tell that you have a healthy ego so I won't pull anything unflattering." She winked to acknowledge Amethyst's reference to "ugly bridesmaid dress syndrome."

"Yes, I want my friends to look beautiful."

Lucy smiled then turned to Amethyst. "Will your hair color change for the wedding?"

"Why? Is it wrong? Julie, do you want me to change it?"

"Of course not."

"No," Lucy spoke gently, "I just want to find a dress that flatters your coloring. The bouquet? Have you decided what it's to be?"

"Red roses with a few white stephanotis and silver twigs."

"Brilliant." Looking at each woman in turn, she mused, "Deep reds to match the roses and because it works with most skin tones—silver accents—something that works for the petite woman as well as the tall one and in stock because time is of the essence." She drummed her fingers against her thigh. "I've got just the thing."

As Lucy hurried away, the four women and Estelle watched her with great interest. Choosing the right dress was more than her job, the woman had a gift and a calling. When she returned, with an armful of deep red, there was a satisfied gleam in her eye, and she did a little dance step.

"Try these."

Amethyst followed Lucy into the dressing room

For the next several minutes, Julie heard rustling and giggling noises from the dressing room then it was quiet. Finally, Gustavia called out, "Hey, Jules. Turn around and don't peek." It was easier to humor her than argue so Julie did as she was asked.

"Okay, now you can look."

Julie spun around, and when she saw the others, her mouth dropped open. Cocktail length chiffon gathered at each shoulder then skimmed across a molded bodice to fall in tiny pleats toward a cinched in waistline banded in silver, then flared back to a flirty, knee-length hem. Artfully posed, each woman looked like a Greek statue come to life. The deep, almost wine red flattered every skin tone and did not clash with Amethyst's vividly colored hair.

113

"Lucy, you are a genius. These are perfect."

Half an hour later, they were back in Beth's shop thanking her for sending them to Lucy, and all four dresses were stowed in the back of Julie's car. Gustavia knew a seamstress in Oakville who could handle hemming Amethyst's dress.

"**Post-wedding**-dress-buying movie marathon suggestions?" Julie asked.

"Father of the Bride, My Big Fat Greek Wedding, Runaway Bride." Gustavia was quick to come up with a list.

"27 Dresses, Wedding Planner, and Wedding Singer." Amethyst chimed in.

"Six movies? That's too many, pick three and we'll make a night of it—Tyler and Reid can entertain themselves this evening."

Gustavia volunteered to go out for supplies since a movie marathon required popcorn, chocolate, and wine. At least.

"Let me grab a coat, and I'll go with you," Amethyst volunteered knowing none of them should be going out alone.

"No, stay. I'll take the dogs with me."

"I don't like it."

"Bad idea."

"No." Julie and Kat spoke at once.

"I'm not scared of Logan. He messes with me, I'll kick him so hard he'll taste his fiddly bits."

At her words, a chill ran up Kat's spine bringing with a sense of foreboding. "Don't be foolish, Gustavia," she admonished.

"She won't be alone," Kat heard Estelle say in her head. "I'll go along, keep an eye on her. She'll never know."

Before anyone else could argue the point, Gustavia was up and out the door calling Lola and Fritzie to follow her.

CHAPTER FOURTEEN

Deep shadows fell in soft pools of darkness at the edge of the tree line bordering the farthest section of the parking lot. Logan huddled and hunched in that darkness watching shoppers wheel carts of groceries to their cars.

Waiting—he remembered what he was doing here—waiting for Gustavia to come out. Even in his thoughts, her name sounded like a sneer. She was a crystal-wearing, new age freak and she had cost him everything. Everything. He hated her, so he waited and planned.

Every time the door opened, his tongue darted out to swipe over lips cracked and peeled from spending too much time outdoors. He had a vague memory of staying in a warm cabin once but not where or when. During the rational moments, he knew he had slipped over the edge. He didn't remember stealing this car or driving it here, but he must have done both.

Time had become twisted and turned back upon itself. Hours passed like minutes and sometimes days felt months long. Yesterday it had been summer-warm, but last night, autumn had begun to blow its cooling breath down his neck. He remembered shivering in the dark, the white plume of his breath like a cloud of smoke rising toward the velvet-blue sky.

He needed a blanket. Julie kept the spare blankets in that chest at the foot of her bed. Thinking of her always brought the blackness—made it swim up from inside him until it sucked him under.

What was inside of him barely kept itself from chortling gleefully at seeing Gustavia stride out of the store alone. The depth of corruption and blackness occupying Logan's body surged over his mind to steal away every good memory until he perceived nothing but emptiness, pain and the hunger for revenge.

By the time Gustavia checked out, the parking lot was nearly empty. A feeling of unease stole over her as the hair on the back of her neck prickled. Surreptitiously she glanced around and saw no one near, but the sensation of being watched was still strong. She walked around the car to pop the trunk and stow the groceries inside.

Logan was out there, she would have staked her life on it. Using her body to block him seeing what she was doing, she grabbed the tire iron. She could almost feel his hot breath on her neck. When she turned around, he was there. The Logan standing before her was not the man she had known. There was something twisting his features into a mask of evil. His eyes glittered with darker intentions.

"Hello, Gustavia." His voice, too, was altered—deeper, more gravelly and she noticed the trace of an accent she had never heard before. Concentrating quickly, even in the low light of dusk, she could see his aura was a roiling black mess with only a hint of color. Whatever had overtaken the man—whether it was an earthwalker, ghost, or his own thirst for revenge—was operating on pure malice.

In the car, both dogs were lunging and barking madly. Lola smelled his scent and recognized him as enemy—the one she had tangled with before. Still, locked inside, there was nothing she could do but raise the alarm, so she continued to bark.

"Logan." She managed to keep her voice even. Maybe she could appeal to that part of him that still clung to the tiny bit of color in his aura. "It's not too late, you can stop this right now; walk away before it goes too far. I know there's a decent man inside there somewhere." She didn't believe that for a minute; she had always despised him, her gut instincts telling her he was not a good person. But, there were levels of wrong and being a lying schemer was a far cry from kidnapping and possibly murdering her.

Keeping her focus trained on his aura, she saw a brief flare of color as his face shifted, only for a second, back to the man she had once known. He choked out one word, "Sorry," before the color was consumed by blackness and hate settled back over his features.

It hadn't worked. She still held the tire iron, and she was not as helpless as he might think. Dropping into a defensive pose, she prepared to fight.

He lunged, and she defended, delivering a straight punch followed by a round kick that broke his nose and rocked his head back. The dark fury of the earthwalker rose up, and he came at her again. She fought bravely but her Krav Maga techniques were no match for the force inside him that continued far past the bounds of his physical body, and he finally wrested the tire iron away from her, whirled around, then brought it down upon her head.

Dazed and in pain, but still clinging to consciousness, Gustavia lay on the ground and remembered Amethyst had once said that anything done with great intention left an aura imprint, so she concentrated on leaving some of her energy in this place.

She felt him pull her up but was unable to resist as he dragged her the short distance to his car and threw her into the back seat before leaning in to secure her wrists with a short bit of rope. She struggled and even managed to get in another kick before he punched her in the face.

Pain bloomed across her cheek as his fist connected, but instead of subduing her, as he wanted, it only made her more determined to thwart him. Feigning unconsciousness, she closed her eyes and slumped in the seat.

He had her now, and he'd get the other one, too. Somewhere inside, what was left of Logan despaired that he had given in to the insanity that possessed him. There was little trace left of the intelligence that had allowed him to craft a con, to act a part and fool a mark. He had given himself over to the darkness, and the darkness had eaten him whole.

Thankful her ruse had fooled him, Gustavia tried to connect her energy through the car to the ground beneath. If it worked, Amethyst, with her new power level, might be able to follow the trail and find her.

It was a slim hope, but since there was nothing else she could do, it had to be enough.

When the car stopped, hoping for some kind of opening to get away, she forced her body to remain limp. Maybe she could use the element of surprise against him. She felt him grab her feet and drag her forcefully out onto the ground. Even though her head slammed against the edge of the car floor on the way down, Gustavia sent another burst of energy into the ground then, when Logan leaned down to pick her up, lunged up and rammed her aching head into his gut.

He let go of her, dropping her heavily down on the gravel drive and stumbled back as she twisted and turned in an effort to stand. Even with her hands tied behind her back, she might be able to do some damage, but before she could make any progress, he delivered a vicious kick to her head.

That was the last thing she remembered until the persistent sound of water dripping finally penetrated her consciousness. Slowly, painfully, she eased into skull-pounding awareness.

Gustavia opened her eyes then quickly closed them again as

even the low level of light in the room felt like sharpened swords stabbing into her brain. Nausea, a greasy grind in her belly, she breathed shallowly to minimize the pain, taking stock as best she could.

The surface under her cheek was soft and rough at the same time. It smelled musty and unused. Maybe it was a bed, maybe some kind of cot; she couldn't tell.

Lying on her stomach, Gustavia gently tried to shift her shoulders into a more comfortable position to ease the aching pull of muscles and realized her arms were now secured behind her.

Each movement brought back the pounding in her head, and she felt every single ache left over from the fight, but still, she struggled against bonds that only tightened with each attempt until finally the relentless pain overwhelmed her again and took her back under.

Helplessly, Estelle watched Logan stalk Gustavia in the parking lot. She tried to yell out a warning but something, some force stopped her, froze the words in her throat before she could utter them.

Panic mounted as she watched for long moments while he moved stealthily closer and closer. She saw the short conversation, the desperate fight, and the final outcome as Gustavia was outmatched by Logan's manic disregard for his own safety.

Logan hadn't come away unscathed either. He had not counted on Gustavia's ability or willingness to fight, and Estelle was sure he was leaving with a broken nose.

Estelle saw him pull Gustavia from the ground and drag her the short distance to his car where he shoved her into the back seat. She saw Gustavia give him that final kick and heard the sound of fist meeting face. She watched him bind Gustavia's hands, shove her limp body across the seat. Then he turned toward Estelle, and she finally saw through the physical barrier to what was inside. With a last malevolent glare at Estelle, he slid inside, slammed the door, and drove away.

Struggling against the force that bound her, Estelle wanted nothing more than to follow, to see where he would take Gustavia. Instead, she was rooted to the spot, unable to take action and it was not until the car was long out of sight before she was finally released. By then, it was too late to follow so she turned her focus back toward Hayward House and help. She sensed Tyler was closer, right down the street.

This was one of those times when it would have been nice to have Julius around. His greater experience with being in spirit form might have given him an edge. The only positive thing that had come out of this was that she had both seen and gotten a sense of the earthwalker. She hadn't known that ghosts could shiver until she felt that cold attention focused on her. She was still shaking from the experience as she concentrated on Tyler to locate his exact location.

CHAPTER FIFTEEN

Heedless of whether or not anyone might see her, Estelle abruptly appeared next to Tyler in the bar where he and the other men were playing pool. It was dark enough that only one other patron noticed and he had enough alcohol already in him to doubt what he was seeing.

"He's taken Gustavia." She announced to the group.

Zack paled but immediately shifted into cop mode. "Where? Tell me what happened."

Estelle laid it out for them, told them where to find Gustavia's car and which direction Logan had gone when he had driven away with her. The only thing she held back was any mention of the Earthwalker. Zack had not seen her shimmer into the room and now was not the time to open up that particular conversation.

"I'll call Julie and let them know." Tyler pulled out his phone.

"No, you go with Zack, help Finn. I'll go tell them. You find her."

"Tell them to stay at the house, safe."

Estelle shot him an arched eyebrow. "Have you met your fiancée and her friends? You know that's not going to happen. I'll bring them to you; it's safest when you are all together anyway."

Before he could protest, she stepped around the corner where Zack would not see her and vanished.

The four men wasted no time covering the short distance

from the bar to the grocery store; Zack called dispatch and relayed his orders. Every officer in the vicinity was called into action. Some to set up roadblocks, others to organize the search. Following protocol with hot fury running through his veins was the hardest thing he had ever done. All Zack wanted to do was find his sister and see her safe. Well, that and take Logan Ellis apart with his bare hands.

Flashing past the gazebo and wishing Julius was back from his mysterious errand; Estelle zipped into the house and nearly shrieked the news, "Logan's got Gustavia. He grabbed her from the parking lot, and there was nothing I could do to help."

"I'll call Tyler." Julie pulled out her phone as she stuffed her feet into the first pair of shoes she could find.

"No need. I just came from there. The men want you to stay here where it's safe," Estelle explained knowing full well that option was not on the table.

Sure enough, Amethyst snorted, "Like we'd just sit here when Gustavia is in trouble. Never happen." She quickly helped Kat with her things and the three women were out the door before two full minutes had passed.

"Where are they?" Julie asked as she slid behind the wheel.

"Parking lot behind the grocery store."

During the short drive, Estelle described for the grim-faced women everything that had happened then said to Kat, "Do you mind?"

Kat knew exactly what she was asking. Estelle wanted her to act as channel so she could remain available longer than her energy normally allowed. "I was thinking the same thing," and she opened herself to let the spirit slide inside. To conserve energy, Estelle stayed in the background speaking to Kat rather than through her.

"We'll find her. It will all be fine." Amethyst kept repeating the words almost as if to reassure herself they were true.

Flashing lights greeted the women as they pulled into the parking lot. Jumping from the car, they raced to the epicenter of the activity.

Zack had already found Gustavia's car keys and released the two dogs. They were now stashed in his cruiser.

Under the harsh glare of the temporary lighting set up by the police, Amethyst saw Zack crouched down to investigate some drops of blood on the pavement. Hoping the blood was not Gustavia's she checked his aura, fear swirled through with anger. Some of the blood did belong to Gustavia; her aura surrounded a few drops but most was surrounded by darkness.

What made Amethyst swear under her breath was the one thing she never expected to see—Gustavia's imprint, clear as day. Even under attack, the woman had had the presence of mind to funnel energy into the ground.

Amethyst could barely breathe. Here was the perfect situation where her gift could be useful, and she was restrained behind a barrier watching the imprint slowly fade as the minutes ticked past.

An hour crawled by as the six friends watched Zack work alongside his team. Sixty endless minutes of knowing Gustavia was at Logan's mercy. As the second hour began counting down, Amethyst's patience waned. She paced, she stalked the boundary, she watched Zack's expression darken as each incoming report was negative.

Enough was enough. A moment came when she thought no one was paying attention, so Amethyst ducked under the tape and made her way across the parking lot.

Stepping forward, she gently touched Zack on the shoulder and quietly asked him to move aside for just a minute.

"Working here, Amethyst." He shrugged her hand away. "Get back behind the barrier."

"Zack, I know. And I know you're scared. So am I, but I might be able to help."

Running a hand through his hair, Zack impatiently stood and

walked a short distance away where he stared at her, cold fury on his face then gestured for her to hurry. With no other auras to distract her, she could see Gustavia's energy outline as clearly as if it had been pressed into the ground. Leading away from the main part of the imprint was what appeared to be a set of drag marks.

"She was still alert when he dragged her away, or I wouldn't be able to see the auric imprints so clearly," Amethyst assured Zack and raised her voice so the others would hear.

"Okay, you've seen whatever it is you needed to see, now get out of the way and let me work," Zack said, voice dripping with impatience. This woo woo stuff wouldn't find his sister, and that was the priority here.

Backing away from his obvious hostility, Amethyst rejoined her friends and told them what she had seen. Estelle told Kat every detail she could remember, including which direction Logan had taken when he drove away; Kat relayed Estelle's words to the others, and they all brainstormed ideas.

"This is my fault." Julie's voice trembled with unshed tears. "I brought him here. I got her into this, and I let her go out alone."

Knowing it was needed, Amethyst spoke sharply, "Self-recriminations won't help anything now. Any one of us could have gone with her, and we didn't. You think you're the only one blaming yourself? What we need to do is think this through, calmly and logically."

Reid couldn't help admiring the way she took charge; even when he could tell her thoughts were just as frantic as everyone else's.

Face set in lines of worry, Finn agreed. "Amethyst's right and so is Julie. She's the catalyst for everything. Think about it—Julie is the one he really wants and taking Gustavia is only a means to that end. He won't kill her because he'd lose his bargaining chip and he won't go far because he wants us—or at least Julie—to find him. I think this is a trap and Gustavia is the bait."

"Zack has to follow procedure, but there's nothing to stop us from looking for her ourselves." Tyler was ready to do anything to get Gustavia back and not just for Julie's sake. Gustavia was family to him, they all were.

Unsure of his place in the group, Reid spoke up, "Jane, you can see her imprint, is there any way she could have left—I don't know—some kind of energy trail?" It might not work with the block in place, but if there was a chance, it was worth exploring.

"It's Amethyst," she corrected absently. "Maybe. If she intentionally pushed her energy through the car and into the ground—and if the rubber in the tires didn't form some kind of barrier—there might be an energy trail. And if I hadn't botched the handling of my new abilities, I could probably see it," she answered, bitterness coloring her tone.

"Kat, what's the word from Estelle? I know Julius has a way of tuning in to a person's energy, can Estelle do anything like that?" Amethyst asked.

Taking a moment to confer with the spirit resting inside her, Kat replied, "She says that if we get close enough, she can sense Gustavia, but right now, there's nothing she can do. I can see her memory of the fight—and he drove off in that direction." She pointed toward the right-hand parking lot exit.

Amethyst in the lead, the group, walked in the direction Kat had pointed. Nothing—no sign at all. Her heart sank leaving her feeling powerless to help. Tears welled up and threatened to spill down her face. What good did it do to have an enhanced ability if she couldn't control it well enough to access it when she needed to—when it was of vital importance?

Reid couldn't bear for her to be in so much pain, he had only just met Gustavia, but he could see the deep bonds between all four women.

There had to be something he could do to show his support and soothe her nerves. Reid stepped forward and placed a hand on Amethyst's shoulder, gently rubbing at the tension he felt; kneading muscles that were taut, rigid with strain.

At his touch, Amethyst felt his intention to help, and somehow the intensity of his empathy got past the block Galmadriel had placed on her ability. On the pavement, like magic, a tire-wide track of energy appeared. It was faint. It would be hard to follow.

With a deep intake of breath, Amethyst whispered, "I see something. Oh my God. I see something. Kat, I need help. Please, come here. Take my hand.

Confused but willing to do anything to help, Kat did as she was asked and the trail brightened, becoming much easier to see.

"Finn." Reaching out the other hand and gesturing for him to hurry, Amethyst hoped his energy, built on his love for Gustavia, would strengthen her vision.

His hand trembling, Finn did as he was bid, but nothing happened. Maybe his energy and hers were incompatible, or his fear kept him emotionally blocked. Julie, not waiting to be asked and pulling Tyler along behind her, took two steps forward and clasped Kat's other hand, feeding their energy through her, into the bond.

Now the trail stretched into the distance, bright as a beacon.

The ding of a bell sounded in Amethyst's head, vibrating through her body with a deep, resonant pitch. She heard Galmadriel say, "To understand true need, one must first be able to ask for help. This was the first test."

Amethyst actually felt some of the control shift from the angel to her in a rush of energy and strength. There was no time to test whether or not she still needed the influx of energy from the others to see Gustavia's aura trail. That was something she could explore once her friend was safe.

"Finn, you drive, I'll give you directions, and the rest of you, keep your hands on me. We'll have her back in no time."

"First, we need to tell Zack we've got something."

But, Zack was having none of it. Too concerned to listen, he dismissed their news without a second thought. "Go, follow the crazy. You find her, you call me, but I won't be holding my breath." He turned away to bark out a series of orders.

Returning to the group, Tyler said, "We're on our own."

They all piled into Tyler's SUV, Finn driving, Reid, and Amethyst in the front seat while Julie, Kat, and Tyler sat on the edge of the back seat and kept a hand each on Amethyst's shoulder. If Reid's touch was more of a caress, she was too preoccupied to notice. Much.

Finn kept a steady hand on the wheel despite the way his nerves were tuned nearly to the breaking point as he pulled out of the parking lot and headed west. A mile slid by, then two more. Amethyst called for a left turn.

Past the lower end of the lake now, they drove out of Oakville, and the light trail stayed steady. "Finn, turn here." Amethyst pointed to a narrow side road on their left. They followed this for another mile or so before she told him to turn left again.

"Here? This is barely a road." Grass grew long in the center of a dirt track that disappeared into the trees.

"Yes, this is it."

They had only driven a few car lengths before Kat yelled, "Stop. Right now, stop."

Startled by the command, Finn jammed a foot on the brake bringing the vehicle to an abrupt halt.

"You mind not scaring the life out of me?"

"She's close." It was Estelle's voice coming from Kat's lips. "I can feel her. Wait here."

With no warning, Estelle separated herself from Kat and arrowed off into the night.

CHAPTER SIXTEEN

Casting out her awareness, Estelle searched for Logan and the blackness that filled him. She found it and him speeding away from her. Hoping it wasn't a mistake, she zipped toward Gustavia's energy.

The tumbledown house sat at the end of a barely-there, old, dirt driveway. With a speed enhanced by fear, Estelle searched every room. No Gustavia. Still, she could feel the younger woman nearby. Rounding the old building, she found a small shed, almost a shack. Anyone looking for a kidnap victim might have passed it by; he had taken great care to leave everything looking untouched; except for the shiny new lock which gave him away.

Estelle passed through the wall to see a bruised and battered Gustavia lying on a musty old camp cot. One eye a swollen slit, the other looked at Estelle first with disbelief, then with welcome.

"Oh, Gustavia, your poor face."

Her voice husky with tears, Gustavia still managed a watery smile as she said, "Broke his nose—the dirty, rotten son of a..."

"They're nearby—Julie, Finn and the rest. I'll bring them to get you out of here," Estelle interrupted.

"Hurry, before he comes back. Tell them to call Zack; Logan is headed for Julie's house. He's using me as a distraction. He knows everyone would search for me and I had the dogs in the car."

"I'm going to get them, it won't be five minutes. You just hold on." Estelle faded. In her excitement, she forgot to ask Kat permission before rejoining her spirit with that of the medium. Under the circumstances, Kat's forgiveness was instantaneous.

"**Just ahead**, there's an opening in the trees, turn there." Kat directed Finn, then said, "Julie, call Zack. Let him know where we are; tell him Logan is headed for Hayward House. He's planning to break in while everyone is out looking for Gustavia. If he hurries, Zack might be able to catch him."

To Gustavia, it seemed as if time dragged unbearably. Not quite five minutes felt like not quite forever before she heard the crunch of tires. For one wild moment, she thought it might be Logan coming back.

Shaking and breathing shallowly, she tried to quiet her mind enough to listen. When she heard four doors opening and the excited voices of her friends, she called out to them.

"In here. I'm in here." Her voice lacked its usual power, but it didn't matter. She could have whispered or even remained silent and with his senses running high, his radar finely tuned, Finn would have known where she was.

The thin crescent of a waxing moon peeking out from behind wispy, fast-moving clouds only provided a weak light. Finn, the first one to reach the locked door called back impatiently, "Shine the headlights over here."

Tyler wasted no time doing just that.

"Do we have anything we can use to cut that lock?"

Amethyst could hear Gustavia sobbing inside and called out, "We're coming. Hang on."

"I've got a tire iron we can use to pry the latch." Tyler popped the rear gate and rooted around to find something—anything—they could use to get the door open.

"Ah, screw that." Too frantic to wait, Finn reared back and kicked the door as hard as he could. The area around the latch gave off a cracking sound but held firm.

"Let me help," Reid put a hand on Finn's shoulder, "together, now. Ready, go." The added force of two men kicking the door was enough. The dry wood around the latch gave with a crunching sound, and the door flew open. Finn rushed to Gustavia's side. "Oh, baby, your poor face. How badly did he hurt you?" Without waiting for an answer, he turned to Tyler, "Call an ambulance. We need to cut her hands free. Do you have a knife?"

"Hang on, I've got one," Amethyst pulled a very small multi-tool out of her coat pocket. The knife blade was very small but sharp.

In the dim light, she very carefully sawed through the bonds. Gustavia cried out with relief as her arms settled into a more comfortable position.

"You came, I knew you'd find me," adding, "I'm okay, just a bit banged up, jerk knocked me out for a few minutes."

Finn sat beside her, carefully gathering Gustavia into his arms while Amethyst and Julie ran gentle hands over her to soothe but also to check for other injuries.

"Fritzie and Lola? He didn't hurt them did he?" Typical Gustavia, worried about everyone but herself.

"Safe and sound."

Julie made the call to Zack. Then, for the second time in as many months, she called the paramedics. Fury rose up inside her as she cursed Logan and paced back and forth in the small space waiting for help to arrive.

Standing, Amethyst gestured for Kat/Estelle to follow her outside. "Estelle is still with you. I think we should ask her to go back to the house, check what's going on and report back to us."

Kat agreed and took a moment to confer silently with Estelle. She knew the spirit's energy was waning.

"She'll do it. Too bad Julius is off doing whatever it is he is doing; we could use his help right now."

"It's necessary. Inconvenient but necessary." Estelle

prepared to extract her presence from Kat. "I'll be back as soon as I can."

"Go quickly." Kat mentally prepared herself for the darkness that was about to fall over her vision. A small sigh escaped her lips.

Hearing Kat's sigh, Amethyst pulled the woman into a hug. The last several hours had run them all through a gamut of emotions and Amethyst realized they were both feeling shaky. That's how Reid found them. Supporting and comforting each other.

In the distance, sirens wailed—their sounds becoming louder and louder. Zack must have sent reinforcements because it sounded as though more than just an ambulance was headed their way. Her arm still around Kat, Amethyst waited for help to arrive. As she did, she reached back, grabbed Reid's hand, and gave it a squeeze.

His every sense on high alert, Zack heard the soft brush of grass whooshing against the underside of his cruiser. Needing the quiet to think, he had clicked his siren off half a mile back. Maybe he should have left it on because now his mind was producing a series of worse case scenarios even though Julie had assured him Gustavia was safe.

Bumping down the old dirt track, he saw the glow of car lights ahead, and his tension level ratcheted up another notch. None of this was Julie's fault yet somehow she managed to remain unscathed while his sister took the brunt of each attack. And what had she been doing out alone anyway?

Sliding the cruiser to a stop behind the SUV, he braced himself for what was ahead, then slammed his way out of the car.

"Where is she?" Zack all but shouted it.

"In there." Amethyst took his arm less to guide him than to lend a bit of comfort. Surreptitiously, she cleared his aura of some of the darker spots. This was a liberty she would normally never take with someone who had not granted permission, but he needed a clear head right now. Whirling lights on the roof of his car clicked and flashed; the glare of red washing over siding weathered by time and neglect to a silvery gray. She pointed to the shed where Gustavia, surrounded by her friends, still lay on the old cot.

He turned in the direction she was pointing and then stopped, gripping her arm so tightly it was almost painful and in a choked voice asked, "How bad is it?"

"Bruises mostly. He hit her in the face, tied her up. Probably another concussion. She's conscious, fully alert, and aware. She says it looks worse than it feels but I won't lie, it looks bad enough."

Zack nodded twice then squared his shoulders and strode away toward the shed calling back over his shoulder, "Let the dogs out of my back seat before they try to chew their way out, will you?"

Freed from confinement, Fritzie made a beeline for the shed. He knew his owner was in there and she was hurt. He considered it his duty to provide comfort. Dashing through the door, he skidded to a halt and dropped to sit on Julie's feet. Gently rearing up on his hind legs, he placed his front paws on the edge of the cot and laid his nose on Gustavia's shoulder.

Lola, on the other hand, leaped from the car, made three ponderous turns around the shed, head lowered to the ground, nosing the grass to catch a scent and then, on a dead run, took off through the trees.

For a few seconds, Amethyst could hear the big dog crashing through the underbrush, the sounds decreasing until Lola was well beyond hearing distance.

Wretched dog. This day had started out so well but was ending badly.

CHAPTER SEVENTEEN

Something was wrong. Since she had begun actively channeling Estelle, Kat had gotten used to the feeling of, occasionally, not being alone in her body. Except for the first time, when the spirit had taken her over without warning, she had learned how to prepare herself, to reduce the shock when her vision suddenly became clear and then for the disappointment when it, again, faded to black.

If nothing else, Estelle had given her hope that she would eventually regain her sight. When, without warning, she had started seeing and hearing spirit, not even her grandmother, renowned psychic Madame Zephyr, could help Kat overcome her fear. Her refusal to accept seeing spirit eventually translated in an inability to see anything at all. Her doctors, unable to find a physical cause called it hysterical blindness.

The label was disconcerting. All she could picture was one of those Victorian women who inevitably fell into a faint whenever surprised. Those reactions seemed frivolous, and Kat preferred to think her situation was a bit more complex.

Still, now that Estelle had come into her life, literally, there was no denying the fact that her loss of vision had its roots in her psyche. The doctors had been right—there was no physical problem, it was all in her head.

This time, she had felt Estelle leave, but somehow the spirit was still tethered to her energy. Kat's vision dimmed, but instead of fading fully to black, it doubled. She could still see vague shapes around her but, more clearly, she saw Hayward House. Estelle was pulling some part of Kat along for the ride. All she had intended to do was lend the ghost enough energy to complete the task, and now she was having an out of body experience. Or half of one, anyway.

Nervous and disoriented, Kat stumbled against Amethyst. Taken by surprise, the smaller, more petite woman also stumbled. Reid reacting with unerring speed managed to catch them both before they went down in a heap.

"What's wrong?" Amethyst glanced at Kat and what she saw made her take a closer look. "Your aura—wow—it's…I've never seen anything like it. It's half yours and half Estelle's split right down the middle."

"Is that unusual?" Reid asked.

"Usually when she channels I see two full auras, Kat's and then Estelle's in a sort of semi-transparent overlay. Never like this."

"She's not with me, but I'm still with her. I can see Julie's house. Logan's there…" She trailed off.

In the dim, red-tinged glow from Tyler's taillights, Amethyst and Reid exchanged a look.

"Kat, are you alright?"

No answer.

Kat stood, her body rigid and unresponsive.

"What do we do?" Reid asked, "Is this normal? This doesn't seem normal." He knew he was probably babbling like an idiot, but he couldn't help himself. It had been easy to accept that Amethyst could see auras, but kidnappings and ghosts? He was out of his element.

"Shhh. Let me think."

"Think fast, the cavalry is here." The sirens were nearly deafening as the ambulance, whirling lights casting more red shadows over everything, skidded to a halt.

"Stay with her," Amethyst cautioned Reid then strode forward to lead the paramedics to the shed.

Leaving them to their work, Amethyst dragged Julie and Tyler outside. "Let Finn and Zack deal with that, we have another problem. Two other problems actually. Lola's gone. She took off in that direction," she pointed out where the dog had disappeared, "before I could stop her. And to top it off, Estelle went to check on Logan and Hayward House, and it looks like she's taken part of Kat with her somehow." Amethyst led Julie over to where Kat still stood.

The nearly moonless night worked in his favor as Logan crept through the swath of trees between where he had parked the stolen car and Julie's home. This time there would be no dog to stop him, no booby traps, and no ever-vigilant boyfriend to keep him from taking back what was rightfully his.

That thought stopped Logan in his tracks for a minute. Rightfully his? Nothing here was rightfully his and well he knew it. He was under no illusion that he had any right to this house or anything in it. He was a schemer and a grifter, but he had always been honest with himself about his character. The sense of entitlement that had just flashed through him was so alien to his self-perception that it dragged him out from under the thing that rode inside his head—at least for a minute or two.

For a short time, he stood motionless, struggling to retain control and failing. That brief pause was enough to tip the balance.

Estelle arrived first but Lola, who, unconstrained by roads, had run straight through the woods to get here, was only two minutes or so behind. Taking a quick circuit around the place, Estelle knew that two deputies were now concealed on the property. One near the gazebo where he could see the back of the house and the other positioned to watch the front.

If she could keep that foolish dog from scaring him off, Logan was about to walk right into police custody. Quickly, she weighed her options. Showing herself to the police was not one of them. Going up against Logan hadn't worked when she had tried to prevent him from taking Gustavia, so trying that again wasn't going to become part of her plan, either. Seeing him creeping toward the house and hearing the distant crash of the dog in the woods, Estelle realized her only chance was to distract Lola.

The decision made, she zipped toward the dog. "Lola," she hissed, "stop." The dog never slowed; she didn't even veer when Estelle appeared before her. All she could do was watch helplessly as events played out.

Logan broke through the trees and was halfway across the lawn when a growling Lola rounded the corner of the house. If Logan had been in control of his own body, he would have recognized the danger bearing down on him a little quicker. As it was, when almost a hundred pounds of angry dog hit him, he staggered and nearly went down. Lola dodged the man's flashing feet and went for skin, but Logan's unholy luck held once again. Instead of sinking her teeth into his thigh, all the big boxer got was a mouthful of loose clothing. The split second it took her to spit out the shreds of fabric cost Lola her quarry.

The specter inside Logan pushed its energy toward the dog casting the same type of barrier that had immobilized Estelle earlier. It worked that way again. Locked into place by his barrier she could only watch as a bewildered Lola lunged twice then gave up and ran back toward her home and safety while the unearthly energy carried Logan back through the woods well ahead of his pursuers.

When the barrier broke, Estelle's borrowed energy was not strong enough to pull her into the chase and instead returned to the body it had been taken from. Kat staggered and sagged against Amethyst for a moment before speaking. "It's over. He got away again. Lola's safe at home and Estelle won't be back until her energy recharges."

Returning to the farm was no longer an option. Logan couldn't remember why he knew this but was sure it was a fact. The cops had gotten ahead of him and closed off every exit, including the trail he had used last time, leaving him only two choices. Stay up in this tree where he had a bird's eye view of the town and take a chance on falling asleep and then just falling or make use of the caves he'd found near the lake. The blanket, extra clothes, kale, and carrots rescued from the farmhouse were stashed in the woods near the farm, and it was at least an hour-long hike from there to the caves. It would be easiest to stay put, but if he did manage to get to the caves, he could hole up for a couple days, wait for the furor to die down and stay a bit warmer. Maybe even risk a small fire.

Caves.

Caves.

Logan squeezed both temples between palms abraded from living rough. But, the word continued to boom through his head. Rough-textured bark tore deeper into those sore hands during the quick slither down the tree.

Caves.

Caves.

It was only when he obeyed and began to stumble and pick his way through the uneven terrain between the tree and the lake that the incessant repetition eased.

The thing inside him leered.

CHAPTER EIGHTEEN

"She's not going to like it." Tyler tapped his fingers on the tabletop; a sound that irritated Zack's already frayed nerves.

"Are you saying no?" Under any other circumstances, Zack's tone could be mistaken for aggression. Though given the stress Zack had been under, Tyler took no offense.

"Of course not. I was merely pointing out that your sister is unlikely to appreciate this particular bit of interference." Not that he cared one whit. Tyler and Finn were in wholehearted agreement with Zack. Gustavia would not be going home alone once she was released from the hospital. In fact, she would not be going home at all.

Finn spoke up, "She'll have to get over it because I won't have her unprotected." He looked first at Zack and then Tyler. "I'll back you up so we can present a united front." It was the first time he had seen Zack lose that pinched look he'd had on his face since Gustavia had been abducted. "You're going to be the one to tell her, though."

"Then we're in agreement, Gustavia will come here."

"Not just Gustavia. He'll have his sights set on Kat and Amethyst now, too, so I think they would all be better off staying here for a while." Tyler turned to Reid, "You'll handle Amethyst?"

"Count on it."

"I'll go talk to Julie then we'll pick up Kat. Zack, you and Finn go pack up some things for Gustavia and Fritzie. This will all go more smoothly if she comes straight here."

With the matter settled, Zack was finally able to relax. His considering gaze landed on Finn, and for the first time, he noticed how pale the man was under the last of his fading summer tan. If his cop sense was worth anything, he figured it was telling him he would be gaining a brother in law before too many months passed. Kat wouldn't have taken that bet, she didn't like to lose.

On the way out the door, Zack clapped a hand on Finn's shoulder. "I think you should be the one to tell her."

"No way. She's your sister, you do the deed."

The good-natured argument followed them out the door leaving Tyler and Reid to chuckle.

"Good thing you live in a McMansion."

Tyler grinned. "A lot of changes these past six months. It's been a wild ride." Then he sobered. "Some of it has been a little hairy. We could have lost her. If it wasn't for Amethyst..." The consequences would have been disastrous. Zack hadn't been the only one with a sister on the line. Tyler loved her like family.

"Any regrets? Doubts? Cold feet?" Reid wanted to believe life could improve in such a short time; it gave him hope for his own future.

"None. I've made a second family here. Julie is everything."

"She feels the same about you. I'm jealous."

"Any success on that front?"

"No. Maybe. A little. We started something the night she saw Logan before it became all angels and auras. Since then, I haven't been able to get a minute alone with her. You think when she's staying here, I'll have a better chance?"

"If you can talk her into it. Zack is going to have his hands full getting Gustavia to agree, but she's not in any condition to balk. Ammie, now? That's going to take some smooth talking.

She likes living alone up there on that hill, and I think prying her out of her comfort zone is going to be a tough sell." More than, if he knew Amethyst, but better not to say that out loud.

"If she won't come here, then I'll camp outside her door. One way or another, I'm going to protect her."

Amethyst may be stubborn, but she was too kind-hearted to shut him out in the cold. "It's one way of getting her to talk to you."

With a thoughtful nod, Reid headed upstairs to pack. Just in case.

"I'm probably safer here than at Hayward House."

Reid's left eyebrow shot up. "Safer here? Alone? On top of this hill and with winter coming on?" His expression said she was deluded, but those were words he was too smart to let pass his lips. Unmoved, he said, "Pack whatever you need. Do you have a carrier for the cat?"

"What about the dogs? Tommy will be traumatized; he's never been around dogs before. No, I'm staying here. I have clients all week; I can't just take off on a whim."

"You do have a history." The words popped out before he had time to think them through. She treated him to a withering look, which he ignored.

"It's under control. The museum is heated, and Tyler and Finn are planning to rearrange it to give you and Kat each a private place to meet clients. You know there is plenty of space to find a safe place for that cat. If that's your only excuse, it's a flimsy one. The bedroom I was staying in is half the size of this whole place. He will manage."

Patient, but adamant that she would be protected; he waited for her to voice the real reason for staying.

She capitulated, "I know. It's just—this is my home. It's quiet, peaceful. It's my sanctuary."

He had to ask, "From me?" His words were quiet, pain-filled.

"No—oh, no. Nothing like that." She had hurt him, too. Probably more than she had realized at the time.

Laying a hand on his arm and doing her best to ignore the way her heart leaped at even that brief contact, Amethyst said, "Reid, I really am sorry. About everything."

"For what it's worth, so am I."

The urge to kiss her nearly overwhelmed him, but he resisted. Instead, he gave her another option.

"Either get your things together, or I'll be going back out to the car to get mine."

Amethyst frowned then it hit her, he was volunteering to stay here—alone—with her. Mind racing through a myriad of possibilities, she realized her mouth had dropped open in surprise, snapped it shut and said in an exaggerated tone of indifference, "Fine. If that's what you want to do." Her heartbeat sped up.

Reid felt a stomach-jumping, pulse-pounding, excitement and did not wait for her to change her mind. He gleefully made the decision to extend his vacation for a few more weeks. "As your husband, it's my duty to protect you." Maybe reminding her of that was a bad idea but it was nothing short of the truth.

That statement earned him a snort, but his sincerity got him a smile to go along with it. Hope bloomed; maybe they could work things out after all. All they needed was a second chance and some time alone.

The question was whether they were both willing to work for it. Reid knew exactly where he stood on the subject.

Since he was now going to be staying here, Reid looked around his wife's underground abode.

The stucco walls had been painstakingly hand-textured then skillfully painted to resemble sandstone. Curved horizontal bands stood out in shaded relief to resemble layers ranging from rich mahogany through sienna to a pale but warm orange. Small up-lights placed at intervals cast dramatic shadows and highlights to emphasize the graceful arcs and patterns. No art hung in the living room; the walls were enough.

Opposite the front door, a short but wide hallway flanked by narrow storage closets on either side led to the kitchen. Lit by several skylights, what he could see from where he stood looked cozy and warm if ever so small. Glass fronted cabinets displayed her mix and match collection of colorful tableware bought at yard sales, flea markets and second-hand shops. She had indulged her tastes by choosing everything from delicate floral china to chunky stoneware in bright colors and geometric designs.

The honey-colored maple table was flanked by a set of mismatched chairs all painted the same color.

Amethyst loved a good bargain. Her favorite being one where she could rescue a piece then repair, repaint and just generally love it back into usefulness. Recycling and upcycling were passions she shared with Gustavia, and in fact, the two women had met by haggling over an old, broken-down table.

The battle between them had been fierce, but when the dust finally cleared, Amethyst owned the kitchen table that Reid was now admiring, and she had also scored a lifelong friend.

Reid did the math in his head. Unless there were other rooms behind the laundry room, he assumed the hallway doors must lead to a single bedroom and bathroom. Well, at least the sofa looked soft, even if it was at least a foot too short. He'd just have to curl up.

Reading his thoughts, Amethyst said, "Looks like you're on the couch, pal."

He shrugged in acceptance but thought she needn't look so gleeful about it. "I don't suppose it folds out or anything?"

Her wicked grin gave him the answer but did nothing to dim the sense of anticipation growing inside. The sofa would have to do. It was better than pitching a tent in front of her door, something he was fully prepared to do if that was the only way he could protect her.

"Fine. It's fine."

She would have considered trading with him since, at her height, the sofa was a perfect length, but he had expected her to refuse to go with him, even to the point of bringing his things. She hated being predictable.

Reid brought in his bag and went into the compact but surprisingly well-appointed bathroom to unpack his personal care items. As he laid his razor on the counter next to her eye shadow—how many shades of purple did that stuff come in—he couldn't help thinking how long it had been since he'd shared an intimate space with her.

He wondered if her habits had changed in the past three years or if they would slip back into the old routines.

Meanwhile, Amethyst was wondering the same thing. Did he still sleep in his skivvies? Could she handle seeing him all half-naked, eyes blurred from sleep, hair mussed just the way she liked it best? The memory was like a gut punch, swift, and all the more painful because of the possibilities now dangling before her. He still loved her; he had told her he did and she had no reason to doubt his word. Why, then, was she finding it so difficult to open up?

It would be so easy to pick up right where they left off—forget the time apart—but would anything really have changed? She wasn't cut out to be the perfect image of a corporate wife, and it wasn't just about the clothes or hair.

Amethyst was just a name she had chosen. Seeing auras was different.

It had started during a field hockey game in fifth-grade gym class. One minute she had been driving the ball down the field and the next she was flat on her back on the ground, looking up at the gym teacher who was surrounded by a haze of pretty, red color.

She had taken a stick to the shin and gone down, hitting her head on the goal post, after scoring, of course.

The doctors had assured her parents that the auras would fade over time and that they were just a residual effect from the concussion. The doctors were wrong. The auras remained, and before long, she began to see more complex combinations of them, and make connections between people's emotions and the shifting of the colors that surrounded them. She began to see patterns in the swirling colors and to lose herself in their study.

Reid had been the only person—outside her family—who never judged, so they spent a lot of time together.

With no other choice, Jane came to terms with her affliction—stopped thinking of it as such and began to consider it a gift. Okay, so maybe at times it was like opening a brightly wrapped package and finding granny panties inside, but it was the thought that counted. Thank you, universe.

"There must be a story behind this place. Underground houses aren't all that common."

"It used to be a fallout shelter. Two of them actually. They were all the rage in the 1950s, and the original owner found them when he was digging to put a pool in his backyard. They had to rent a crane to get them out of the hole. I bought them for the cost of the crane rental. Really cheap."

Reid walked over to touch one of the walls and discovered that under the cleverly painted sandstone was a plastic wall that curved toward the ceiling. While Amethyst continued, "My uncle owned this piece of property. I think he got it at a tax auction. He planned to fix up the old house but the first winter after he bought it, the whole place collapsed into the cellar hole. When he found out how much it was going to cost to get it cleaned up, he decided to cut his losses and sold me the land for what he'd paid. I talked some friends into helping me clear out the debris, and I sold the granite blocks from the old foundation for enough to install a wastewater system. There was an old well already in place, so with very little digging, I dropped the shelters into the old hole, connected them and buried them for around the cost of a used car. It's small, but it's home."

"How long have you been here? Did all this happen before you left me?"

This discussion was exactly what she had hoped to avoid. Still, she owed him some kind of explanation. "No, of course not. This was two years ago. The first year we were apart, I moved around a lot. Spent some time finding and learning from other aura readers, rented a houseboat for the summer, did odd jobs here and there. But eventually, I needed to put down roots." That it had not been easy for her was evident in the painful hitch of her voice.

It struck him as appropriate and a bit funny, the thought of putting down roots in an underground home. There was something oddly literal about it. However, he wasn't laughing at the knowledge that she had fled the home he provided for her. Not for someone else or even for something better but just to get away from him.

No way was he going to apologize again, though. There was nothing to be gained from endlessly rehashing the past. He would bite his tongue to a bloody pulp before bringing it up one more time. From now on, he would take his cues from her. Let her make the moves for a change. Oh, he still wanted his marriage to work, but for that to happen, they both needed to build back some trust.

"Look," he said, "I know this isn't the best case scenario; me staying here with our history and all the things left unsaid, but I couldn't forgive myself if something happened to you. I don't want to revisit painful memories. We used to have fun together before you started hating me."

"I never hated you," Amethyst spoke with quiet conviction. "Never."

She turned her head as much to draw peace from her view of the lake as to keep him from seeing the unshed tears in her eyes. No, hate was not the right word for what she felt. Not at all.

Finally, with her features carefully schooled to keep him from reading just how much she was affected by his presence, she turned back to him, "Let's make the best of the situation."

He nodded then an awkward silence fell before Amethyst suggested he unpack the rest of his things.

Motioning for him to follow her, Amethyst led the way to her bedroom. Two steps into the room, Reid stopped and let out a low whistle. The room shimmered. That was the only word he could think of to describe it.

Cozily set into the smaller of the two shelters, the bedroom walls curved gently upward to meet at the top in an unbroken arch. Tinted in a variety of colors, iridescent pearl paint washed the walls, each color melting and blending into the next like a watercolor made of subtle light.

In contrast to the flare of color on the walls, the bed was nothing more than a simple platform made from polished pine with a thick mattress covered by a crisp, white duvet.

Unable to help himself, he stepped forward and brushed his hand across the wall, almost expecting the color to feel as liquid as it looked.

"This—it's what you see, isn't it?" He had always wondered,

but she had never been able to teach him to see auras. "It's beautiful."

Without answering, she brushed past him and crossed to the long, low dresser cleanly painted gleaming white. Even though their bodies had barely touched, every point that had made that delicate contact felt energized as she moved through the confined space, she kept her back to him as she yanked out a drawer and began pulling things out to make room for his clothes. Instead of keeping his distance, and letting her maintain the facade that she was unaffected, he stood close, too close and looking down, commented dryly, "This dresser brought to you by the color purple."

"Ha ha." Nevertheless, he was right. In every shade from palest lavender to deepest eggplant, her clothes looked like they had been slapped by the wand of the purple fairy. Slapped hard. Just what she was going for.

Loathe to try squeezing back past him, she pointed to the drawer and waited for him to unpack his bag, which he did by unzipping it and upending it over the empty drawer. With one eyebrow raised, she watched him jam the jeans and tee shirts down and push the drawer closed. Every tiny part of her wanted to fold his things into neat piles, but she resisted.

Satisfied, he turned and left the room as she watched him walk away. There was something about the curve of his calf that had always gotten to her. The man certainly filled out a pair of jeans.

In the bathroom, he pulled open the shower curtain, looked at the confined space, and decided he could make do—if he crouched. Ten minutes later, nursing a bruised elbow that had made contact with the back wall, he stepped out of the torture chamber figuring he was at least marginally cleaner than when he'd stepped in.

The sound of banging pots and pans echoed from the kitchen

148

along with the tearful sounds of stringed instruments. Whistling along, Reid thought, just like old times, and went to rescue her from having to cook. The Amethyst he remembered hated to cook. Clearly, that had changed. His mouth dropped open as he watched those graceful, orchid-tipped hands expertly slice an onion into paper thin rings. The lurch of his stomach marked yet another jarring realization that she'd moved on, changed, and grown during her absence from his life.

Looking up at him, those hands never missed a beat as she tossed the onions into a sizzling pan, then continued to chop more vegetables. Responding to his obvious surprise, she said, "What? I took some classes. Gustavia made me do it."

Shrugging he decided to adapt and so moved into the kitchen to help, seeming to know instinctively where everything was. But it wasn't instinct. It was that even after all this time, their organizational styles still matched so that everything in her compact kitchen was placed exactly where he, himself would have put it.

Without thinking, they fell into a rhythm. A dance.

All the tension slid away as the simple task of preparing and eating a meal occupied their focus.

Maybe this wouldn't turn into a disaster after all.

The smell of buttered popcorn wafted from the bowl between them as Amethyst and Reid struggled to watch a movie. Separate bowls—that would have been a good idea, she thought as electricity shot through the hand that bumped into his for the third time. They were sixteen again, just in the first flush of attraction where every touch, every glance caused a shiver of excitement. Amethyst tried to pay attention to the movie, but she was too attuned to his every movement to follow the plot. She kept her eyes trained on the screen, but he was there, in her peripheral vision, looking all loose and comfortable.

Six inches. If she just moved over six inches, she could rest her head in the spot on his shoulder that had seemed made for her. His arm would slide around her and... *No, just watch the movie*, the angel on her own shoulder admonished. *Why?* The devil on the other replied. *You want him. He wants you. What would be the harm?*

What indeed?

Unaware of the internal struggle going on beside him, Reid was fighting a similar battle of his own. Everything in him yearned to pull her across that couch, settle her on his lap, and ravish her mouth in a kiss that would bind their fates together forever. The thought of her mouth on his stirred a desire so primal, so deep that he was almost powerless to resist. Staying here and keeping his hands off her would be torture. After all, he was no saint.

"Were there many other men?" He heard himself ask the question right along with her and cursed himself for a fool.

"Excuse me?"

Now that he had opened the can of worms, he might as well fish. "You thought we were divorced, you are a beautiful woman, you must have dated."

"I..." She stammered, then decided she might as well be honest. "Yes, I dated other men. Does that make you feel better or worse?"

He ignored the question. "Anyone serious?" It was the last thing he wanted to know, and yet he could not help but ask.

"What are you really asking me? Do you want to know if I slept with other men? Because that's what it feels like you are asking me."

"Maybe I am."

Her eyes searched his face for some indication of what he

wanted to hear, but his expression was unreadable. Inane dialog from the movie played out for a few seconds before she reached for the remote and muted the television. When she turned back, he was still waiting for her answer.

"I dated, Reid. I thought I was single and I refuse to apologize for anything I have done. You can't come back into my life after all this time, dump a huge revelation on me, and expect those years to just vanish."

"Did you love any of them?" He hoped the answer was no, any other answer would probably kill him.

She owed him honesty, and that is what she gave him, "No. I didn't." Total honesty. "None of them was you."

A weight fell from him. He would not ask anything more of her on the subject.

After a moment of awkward silence, she didn't know what else to do so picked up the remote and went back to watching the movie with absolutely no idea what it was about anymore. This time, she kept her hands out of the popcorn bowl—less chance of accidental touching, and she needed the distance.

Then he quietly asked, "Don't you want to know if I looked for someone else?"

Since honesty was the theme for the evening, she treated him to a wry smile. "What makes you think I didn't keep tabs on you? Or to be more honest, there were plenty of people in town who made it their business to tell me any little piece of gossip. So unless you had a clandestine series of girlfriends, I would have heard."

"Oh, I never knew."

"Yeah, well, the perks of suburban living. So, did you?"

"Did I what? Have a clandestine series of girlfriends?"

She shrugged.

"No. I never had the time or inclination. I'm the one who chose to stay married, remember?"

That was the conversation she wanted to avoid, and there was nothing constructive she could say, so Amethyst turned back to the movie, surreptitiously rubbing at her throbbing temple. The discussion had given her a headache.

Banished to the kitchen while Amethyst was busy doing an early morning reading, Reid could see the sofa from where he was sitting. Two nights spent on that torture device had his left shoulder aching like a rotting tooth. He rotated the joint to release some of the stiffness. Not that he had slept much with her in the next room. Every movement she made rustled the sheets, and the noise tightened his body with the need to join her there. He wondered if she was feeling the same.

After his first night there, they had managed to avoid further awkward conversation and begin the process of feeling more comfortable with each other. As it was now, they could talk about anything unrelated to their relationship with easy openness. If they both ignored the sexual undertones, they could get along fine.

Determined to remain optimistic, he pulled out the box of cereal he had bought the day before after he had opened her cabinet to find his options were limited to a box of something that looked like twigs and nuts with a few berries thrown in. A man just could not survive without a few essentials like sugary cereals. Not just for kids, he thought.

The local market had been out of the plain version of his favorite brand so he'd ended up buying the one with berry-flavored bits added in. When Amethyst walked into the room twenty minutes later, he was seated at the table, two bowls in front of him, separating the colored balls from the yellow pillow-shaped pieces.

"Do I want to know what you're doing?" Amusement fought with derision, and the two called a truce; both appearing on her face, as she turned wide, skeptical eyes on him but grinned at the same time.

"They didn't have the plain kind, so I'm making my own." He popped a yellow square into his mouth. "Bah, they're tainted. Tainted, I tell you. They all taste like berry." He poured all of the cereal back into the box, shook it to mix them back together, and poured a bowlful, which he proceeded to eat with great gusto.

"I'm not sure whether to laugh at you or have you committed. Crazy man."

"Want some?"

"No, I've eaten a balanced, adult breakfast."

"Of twigs, nuts, and berries?"

These moments of teasing were a comfort to them both as long as the elephant in the room stayed in his designated corner.

"What's on your agenda for the day?" She changed the subject.

That was a loaded question since there were things he would like to add to his agenda that she clearly wasn't ready for. Ever since the session in his car, he'd had trouble thinking of anything other than a repeat of that moment in a less confined space. Two steps and he could have her in his arms. Fewer than twenty and he could have her in the bedroom. It might as well be twenty miles, though.

"I've got some job offers to look through."

"Anything promising?" Maybe if he went back home, she could get him out of her head.

"I guess that depends on your definition; I've got headhunters chasing me about CEO positions in the industry, but that's not what I want to do."

"You want to go into non-profit work." It wasn't a question. No matter what had happened between them, she knew his dream job was to help people. It was one of the things she loved most about him.

"Absolutely. When Dad started pushing me into the insurance business, its only appeal was that I would be helping people, but that turned out not to always be the case." For the first time since he had arrived, he felt he could open up to her. "In the beginning, it seemed like a reasonable compromise, but it didn't take very long to see that finding ways not to help was the directive. It was killing me."

"Then why did you stay?"

"I applied for other positions for the first six months but never got an interview."

"Do you think Lionel had anything to do with that?" She wouldn't put it past her father-in-law to manipulate his son into staying with the company.

Reid shrugged. He hoped not.

"Have you talked to Tyler about it? He has contacts just about everywhere."

An odd look fitted itself on Reid's face. "I tried, but he brushed me off."

Amethyst frowned, "That doesn't sound like Tyler. At all." She could tell that Reid's feelings were hurt, but there was nothing she could do about that, though the next time she saw Tyler, she intended to corner him and find out what was going on.

CHAPTER NINETEEN

Two weeks passed before Logan had his next moment of clarity. Weak with cold and hunger, he stumbled from his cave sanctuary and made his way back to the road leading out of town. By now, the roadblocks had long come down, and he needed to get back to the city where he still had at least one safe house left and there was a chance of blending into the crowd.

The trip out of the woods was long and arduous for someone with depleted strength. Twice, he fell. Twice, he forced himself to rise and continue on. It was only his highly developed sense of self-preservation that kept him going.

Mile after mile, he trudged until the movement was no longer directed by thought but became automatic and mindless. Logan stumbled through a shallow ditch, onto the pavement and into the path of an oncoming vehicle. The screech of the brakes was the last thing he heard before he fell.

Instinct had him folding his arms over his head for protection, but at that moment, he was too spent to do anything more.

"**Mike. Stop.**" Dolores punched the imaginary brake on the passenger side floorboards and yelled at her husband.

"I see him, woman." His reflexes had already kicked in as he simultaneously slammed the pedal to the floor and reached a hand out to brace her from impact. If the pavement had been wet, it would have been all over for the young man lying in the roadway, but Mike managed to bring the car to a stop mere inches from the prone body.

As one, the couple leaped from their car and rushed to help.

Logan was already struggling to regain his feet when Mike reached out a hand to steady him. The older man's hand was none too steady, and his heart was still beating a hundred miles an hour from the adrenaline. Dolores could barely catch her own breath in the aftermath of fear. She looked around her. What had the young man been doing out here, there wasn't a house for miles and miles. She didn't remember passing any breakdowns on the road, either.

"Close call there, I darned near hit you. What's your name, young fellow?"

"Peter Jenkins, sir. I've been lost in the woods for a few days. Is there any chance you could give me a ride?"

Mike looked the young man up and down. Giving rides to strangers these days was a dicey business. He watched the news, saw the stories and they never ended well for the innocent driver. Still, Peter looked half-starved and weak as a kitten. Dolores, standing behind Peter, was shaking her head and Mike sent her a quelling look.

"You'll ride up front with me so I can keep an eye on you, but first, you turn out your pockets so I can see you're not carrying a weapon of any kind."

Logan was unarmed and in his present state, not much of a threat to anyone so he complied. For once, instead of getting angry, he was just thankful for the help.

"I promise, I won't be any trouble. I just need to get back to the city." He pulled his pockets out to prove he was unarmed and climbed into the passenger seat. He looked half-starved, so Dolores offered him the granola bar she always carried in her purse, then watched him suspiciously from the back seat as he practically inhaled the food then fell asleep.

CHAPTER TWENTY

The solstice was coming up quickly, and with everything happening at once, everyone had all but forgotten about the key and whatever it might unlock. The clues Julius had given to Amethyst seemed like vague nonsense. Something about looking where the light bent, and something about it being in the last place they looked, whatever that meant. Without him constantly prodding, the time slipped away quickly.

As daylight fell like a curtain through the skylight above her bed, Amethyst had the uncanny feeling, even in her sleep, that she was being observed. Prying one eye open, it was met by the withering stare of a cat in a mood. Tommy sat on the duvet, his face no more than two inches from hers as he tried to communicate whatever deep-seated feline emotion he was feeling at the moment. He felt entitled to them, after all, with his strenuous life of sleeping and keeping his toes meticulously clean.

Casting her sleep-drugged mind over the options, Amethyst knew he had been fed and watered the night before, and it was too early for him to be prowling for food now, anyway. Preferring to do his business outside, he rarely availed himself of the indoor commode, so it was unlikely to need a cleaning.

"What?" She asked him not expecting an answer.

"He's trying to warn you that you have a visitor," Julius spoke from the doorway where he stood, his eyes respectfully averted.

"Oh for the love of...don't you have descendants you can haunt? I need my beauty sleep." She wrinkled her nose while asking the rhetorical question. "Go on into the kitchen, I'll be there in a minute," she ordered. "Oh, and put the kettle on for tea."

"Funny," he retorted then grumbled under his breath, "I could if I wanted to. Useless waste of energy, though."

Dressed and mostly awake, Amethyst wandered into the kitchen to find Reid wearing nothing but the jeans he had hastily pulled on. His bare chest drew her attention, but it was the cup of her favorite tea in his hand that she wanted most at that moment. Inhaling the scent of mint, she woke up just that little bit more and decided he made a pretty picture standing there while he and Julius made small talk. By now, the presence of ghosts and angels were as commonplace to him as they were to her.

Amethyst reached for the jar and used the honey dripper to sweeten her tea then gulped down a mouthful. "How was the trip to—where was it Galmadriel sent you?" She frowned as she tried to remember. It was too early in the morning for rational thought.

Julius ignored the question for the moment and asked one of his own.

"What have you done about those clues I gave you? The solstice is coming up, and it's imperative you find the key."

His words pinned her to the spot; she felt like a schoolgirl called to the principals' office. She slid a glance over at Reid who shrugged, grinned, and shook his head to indicate she was on her own. Way to be helpful, she thought as she blinked and tried to form a coherent answer.

Clearing her throat, she answered, "Well, with everything that's happened, we just..." She couldn't meet the ghost's eyes, "forgot about it." The excuse sounded as lame as she had known it would and Julius was unimpressed.

"Forgot about it?" His voice rose, and he appeared ready to launch into what her mother would have called a conniption.

Before he could do more than sputter, she added. "Don't worry, we'll figure it out. I'm on the case, and Reid will help me. I'll call Julie first thing, and we'll go over there and start looking for the last place in the world where light bends or whatever."

Judging by the stern look on his face, Julius was not exactly pleased by her answer, but there was little he could do about it.

"Now, what happened with Galmadriel?"

Again, he ignored the question in favor of one of his own.

"Did you accept her offer? Are you a reader now?"

"Have you been completely out of touch? Even with Estelle? A lot has happened."

Anxiety wrote itself in the deepening lines of his face, now that she was paying attention, she could see he looked worn, tired and haggard as he motioned for her to continue. What on earth could a ghost be doing that would make him look so tired?

"If you would please be so kind as to enlighten me?"

"Yes, I accepted my gift, but there were complications," and she explained about the shifting auras and the three tests while he listened with barely contained patience.

"And the tests, have you passed them?"

"Only one so far. When Logan kidnapped Gustavia, and I asked for and accepted help from the others to find her energy trail."

"Did he hurt her? The circus girl, is she all right? And Julie?"

"Gustavia will be okay. He beat her up, but we found her in time and Julie's fine." He had come here first—without even checking in at Hayward House, Amethyst realized. But, why?

More gently this time, she asked, "Julius, where did Galmadriel send you?"

"On a trip through the past to find the origin of his hatred."

"Logan's?" Reid finally spoke. According to the story, Logan had only latched on to Julie as a means to an end, that end being sole ownership of Hayward House and its surrounding property.

"No, not Logan's, he's left town, by the way. This goes back well beyond him or..." Julius trailed off and remained quiet long enough for Amethyst and Reid to exchange a questioning look. "I'm only going to tell this once. I'll round up Estelle if you would be so kind as to gather your friends. Call for me when you're ready."

Before she could protest, he was gone.

She threw her hands up in the air. "No, thank you, Julius, I didn't have any clients today. Sure, I can just alter my life to suit you. No problem at all." Her sarcastic tone was belied by the twinkle in her eye. Julius reminded her of her own grandfather, and she had a soft spot for both of them.

"I assume you did have work-related things planned," Reid said as he pulled eggs, veggies, and cheese from the fridge; she wasn't going anywhere without breakfast.

"Yes, but no clients. I get a lot of downtime around the holidays, but it picks up again once the winter sports season starts in mid-January. Then it gets busy again from spring through fall."

"Anything I can do to help?"

"I just need to print off some shipping labels and invoices, seal up the envelopes, and make a run to the post office." Her line of guided meditation packages sold well this time of year. Most people downloaded them in MP3 format for digital music players, but there were always a few orders for the CD version. A spate of orders had come in during the week so she would be detouring into town on her way to Julie's and Julius would have to live with that.

With Gustavia and Kat staying at Hayward House temporarily, they were already on the spot. Kat was just finishing up a mid-morning reading, and Gustavia was working on the final edits of her latest children's book. Finn was also there to reinstall the baseboard molding in the room where Julie and Tyler would be getting married.

His wedding gift to them had been to refinish the parquet floors that were paint-spattered from the time Estelle had used the room as a studio. Now sanded and coated in a warm honey with red overtones, they looked amazing.

"I could drop you at the house and go to the post office for you," Reid offered. "I'm not really part of the crew, so it doesn't matter if I'm there and I get the feeling Julius isn't the most patient of—I wanted to say people, but I guess spirits would be the better term."

"He woke me up; he can wait his turn," then a thought came to her, "unless you don't want to be there."

Tension crept into the car until he reached over and laid a hand on hers. "I want to be there. I was just trying to be sensitive and supportive."

"Um…hm. I see. I thought for a minute you had something against hunting for treasure. Frankly, that might just call your manhood into question," she teased.

"I'm all man. If I was a doll, I'd be G.I. Joe."

"Not Ken? He was the pretty one."

"Nope. Got me the Kung Fu grip and everything."

"Glad we cleared that up—I think."

The Post Office occupied one of the smallest storefronts in town. With limited counter space, the line stretched out the door so Julius would be waiting a bit longer than expected.

Several exiting patrons greeted Amethyst warmly as they passed by. The first time, she stumbled over introducing Reid. Did she call him her husband? Her friend? Finally, she decided to introduce him by name. Judging by his smirk, he found a great deal of amusement in her discomfort.

Amethyst ignored speculative looks even when Emily Snowden glanced back then surreptitiously pulled out her phone to send thumbs flying over the texting keyboard. The woman was the most notorious gossip in town, and it came as no surprise several minutes later when jewelry store owner, Tamara, stepped out of her shop and walked purposefully toward the Post Office.

"And there's the famous Oakville grapevine in full swing." Amethyst murmured to Reid before greeting Tamara warmly. Tamara had managed to get a photo of Logan vandalizing Gustavia's car a few months back, and Amethyst was not about to treat her shabbily now. Besides, Tamara was relentless in her pursuit of town knowledge, ignoring her would be a pointless activity.

"Introduce me to your friend." Tamara eyed Reid with a twinkle in her eye. She might be a gossip but was never malicious with it. Amethyst did as she was told then shamelessly left the man to his own devices when the line moved her inside. His look of panic as Tamara pulled him from the crowd was priceless.

By the time her packages slid into the bin waiting for dispatch, Tamara had extracted everything but his shoe size from Reid. Well, his shoe size and the fact that he and Amethyst were married. He barely managed to keep that one to himself.

Still, he was thankful when she returned and rescued him from Tamara's clutches. Amethyst thought he looked shell-shocked.

"I think she used a truth ray on me. I spilled my guts to that woman, and it took less than five minutes. She should be an interrogator or something." He caught the look she slanted him. "I didn't tell her our big secret. But another two minutes and I'm pretty sure she would have gotten it out of me. "

Maybe that wouldn't have been so bad.

"...and then Julius said to call him when we were all together," Amethyst explained as Julie and Gustavia glanced from her to Reid with speculation written all over their faces. If Reid hadn't been standing right there, they would already be grilling her about how things were working with him living in her tiny house. She ignored them and called out for Julius.

"No need to shout, I'm right here. What took you so long?"

Biting down on the words—because I have a life—they just seemed too mean, she gestured for him to get on with whatever it was he had to say. Estelle tried but failed to hold back a smile because none of these women found Julius the least bit intimidating when he was in a black mood. It tickled her to see him bluster when he thought he wasn't getting the proper level of respect.

"First things first," he began, "have you found the key?"

"Not yet."

"Well, why not?"

No one wanted to confess to forgetting the key.

"Wedding plans."

"Getting ready for Christmas."

"Deadline for my manuscript."

Julius considered none of these a worthy excuse for shirking duty. "Finding that key is imperative. Everything hinges on your completing this task."

"I'm sorry. We'll get on it right away." Chagrin turned Julie's face a delicate shade of pink, and she vowed to treat the matter with the urgency it deserved.

"It would help if you explained what 'everything' is." Gustavia gently probed for information without expectation. Whatever authority had allowed Julius and Estelle to be here kept a tight rein on their releasing any secrets.

"I've told you all I can about that; you'll have to be satisfied with the story of my journey back through time."

His words piqued everyone's interest, so they settled in to listen to his story.

"When I was sent back here, it was with a simple directive—to help my family find what had been lost. I don't think the powers-that-be were counting on it taking so long. For certain, they had no inkling that Logan's involvement would pose such a problem. Left to himself, he would have moved on by now. Unfortunately, he has not been left to himself—he has become a vessel for an Earthwalker."

"Galmadriel told me that already. She said Earthwalkers are spirits that choose darkness." Amethyst interrupted his narrative.

Julius raised an eyebrow at the interruption.

"As I was saying, Logan has become a vessel, and I was sent to find the event that caused the Earthwalker to turn from the light." He paused for long enough that Estelle gently prodded. "And did you find the event?" The look on his face was unreadable. Julius was finding it difficult to tell his story for some reason, but he began anyway.

"My grandfather, it turns out, was something of a scoundrel in his youth. He grew out of it to raise my father with a keen sense of right and wrong—most probably because my grandmother would have tolerated nothing less—but before he married her, he had a rival for her affections. A young man named Billy—I didn't catch his last name. The two fought bitterly over her affections, though it hardly mattered since my grandmother disliked Billy intensely. Still, for some reason, he thought he was a contender for her hand and sought to win her for himself."

"In the end, the two men played a game of cards, agreeing that the loser would bow out. My grandfather won, but Billy insisted that he had cheated and hatred grew within him. He vowed revenge, but on the day my grandparents married, Billy went to sea with a merchant ship named *Indestructible*."

"The next year, my father was born, and my grandparents moved from Indiana to South Carolina where my grandfather worked, first in shipping then later as a trader. He became comparatively wealthy and eventually moved his family here, to Hayward House."

This seemed to be the end of his story.

"So, you think Billy is the Earthwalker?" Amethyst mused.

"And you think it is possible that Billy is one of Logan's ancestors?" Tyler felt the story click into place. That had to be it.

"I do. You'll do the research?" Now that his contribution was over, Julius began to fade, and before Tyler could answer, he was gone.

"Where do you usually find things?" Gustavia sat with her sprained ankle propped up on a large tie-dyed pillow, her face a rainbow of healing bruises. To celebrate the healing process, she had braided Band-Aids into her hair. Every size and shape fluttered around her face. After wondering how one added bandages to a hairdo, Amethyst gave in and checked for herself. Thread. They were sewn into the braids.

Julie repeated, "*Where do you usually find things?* What kind of clue is that? It's the worst one yet, and we've left it until the last minute." Now she was getting nervous. The stakes must be higher than she realized to keep Julius so agitated.

Getting information piecemeal frustrated her no end.

"It reminds me of a joke my grandmother used to tell. Something about the thing you are looking for will always be in the last place you look. When I was a kid, I didn't get it until she finally explained that if you find the thing you are looking for, you stop looking so whatever you found was in the last place you looked." Reid mused.

"Good one, but not at all helpful." Tyler had his laptop out and was either doing some kind of Internet search or making one of his famous lists.

Reid's words triggered a fleeting thought, but Amethyst couldn't seem to catch hold of its tail. Standing, she paced across the room in short strides, but the thought remained elusive. Last place you looked. She knew that was the clue and that Julius tended to speak more literally than figuratively. Following that line of thinking, the last place they had looked had literally been the chandelier because that had been the location of the last hidden cache.

"I've got it—or I think I have." She turned and hurried from the room followed by everyone except Gustavia who yelled, "Hey. Don't forget me." She grabbed for her crutches.

Finn returned with a sheepish grin, "Sorry, got caught up." He took the crutches from her and, instead, carried her up the stairs where they found Amethyst gazing up at the chandelier.

"That's the last place we looked. I think we need to look at it again."

Finn and Reid went out to set up a ladder while Tyler rounded up the glass lenses that triggered the lowering mechanism.

Their last batch of hidden heirlooms, family jewelry and a nice collection of pearls and gems, had been cleverly hidden above the chandelier. Using his unique set of skills, Julius had rigged up a concealed winch that only switched on when a series of glass lenses were inserted into the dentil molding on the front of the Greek-style architrave over the porch.

You had to give Julius credit for being inventive. Of course, since the man had made his fortune as an inventor, it made sense.

The jewels they had found, though, had not been listed in any family records that Julie had ever seen and Julius had not supplied any further information about them. Their estimated value made Julie a relatively wealthy woman.

In a few short minutes, the sound of the mechanism whirred above them, and the chandelier descended from the ceiling. While they waited for the men to return, Amethyst took a moment to tune in on any aura surrounding the chandelier. Even with the angel's block, most everything was surrounded with faint color. The chandelier was no different.

Concentrating a bit deeper, she began working her way through the layers of color attached to the fixture. Julie and Tyler's overlapped each other as always and were easiest to spot since they were the brightest. Just to see what would happen, she made a brushing motion with her hand, and to her surprise, they slid away.

Gustavia saw what Amethyst was doing and gestured for the others to watch.

Next were Gustavia and Finn's auras, also bound together, they both whisked away as one. Kat's was the hardest to remove because her aura was tied to both Julius' and Estelle's. But with some extra concentration, the two women's auras flowed away like cobwebs before a broom leaving only the light patterns distinctive to Julius.

With a hand gesture similar to turning up a volume knob, Amethyst increased the aura's depth and brightness. And that's when she hit pay dirt. The increasing depth caused older aura signatures to deepen and become more visible.

The oldest were attached to the body of the fixture where a closer look at the intricate filigree patterns etched into the metal proved to be script of some kind.

"Look at this, I've found something," her normally deep voice rose an octave in excitement. "I think it's writing of some sort, but I can't read it."

Tyler took one look and knew exactly what he was seeing. In time-honored tradition, he had played at being a spy as a boy. This was one of the oldest spy tricks he had used. Mirror writing.

Looking around the room, he found exactly what he needed, the handheld mirror from an antique dresser set and holding it at the proper angle began to read, "Glass can reflect, or it can bend light. 3:15."

Among the sparkling crystal drops hanging from the chandelier were seven small prisms hidden in plain sight, but hidden so well that anyone not specifically looking for them might never notice.

Now they had the key and time of day. It was an excited group that trooped into the room with the window.

Reid noticed Amethyst hanging back behind the others, a bemused look on her face.

"You okay?" Concern painted a deep crease between his eyes.

"What? Yeah, I'm fine." Finding a way to control the auras felt like it had come from the same pool of calm she tapped when meditating. She hadn't even thought about what she would do, just let that calm wash over her and it all happened from there. Easily. Naturally.

"Could have fooled me. I can see your hands shaking."

"They are?" Holding them up, she flipped her hands from front to back and realized he was right, they were. "Oh. I guess they are. Did you see that? I controlled it." The urge to jump up and down overcame Amethyst, but she settled for a loud whoop. "It was amazing. I didn't even think about what to do, and my instincts took over. I could see the layers of color, but more importantly, I could see the separation points between them." She grabbed his face and planted a big smacking kiss on his lips then wiggled her hips in a victory dance down the hall as he laughed and watched.

One of the prisms fit perfectly in the wire holder that popped out of the frame, but no amount of searching turned up so much as a second hidden holder, much less six more of them. After an hour of searching, they gave up and headed back downstairs where Julie suggested everyone stay and help decorate their Christmas tree.

CHAPTER TWENTY-ONE

Reaching for the same red ornament, Reid's warm hand brushed against Amethyst's smaller one. Catching her eye, he deliberately turned the accidental touch into a caress that felt like fire running across her skin. She froze, enjoying the sensation. It had always been like that between them, each touch kindling the flames of need.

Remembering that she wasn't supposed to want this anymore, she pulled away but not before he had seen the intake of breath that betrayed her. She turned and hung the glass bauble on the tree before accepting the cup of eggnog Julie handed her. The timing could not have been better; her mouth was dryer than desert sand.

When he moved close and leaned in to hang a crystal angel on a lower branch, she let her breath flow across the sensitive part of his neck. He shivered. Two could play at that game. When his eyes flew to hers, she quirked a brow at him, and it was on.

Touch for touch, they fanned the flames, built the pressure to a screaming level that could only be released by one thing. The one thing they both wanted more than they wanted to breathe. The one thing they both wanted to avoid.

So they did the dance.

By the time the tree was decorated, and it was time to leave, the tension was so strong between them that neither spoke during the ride home. Her continued silence had Reid planning a cold shower and another night cramped on the tiny couch.

Amethyst was the first one out of the car, and as he watched her walk down the path to her front door, he wished things could be different. He certainly wasn't expecting what came next. He had barely closed the door behind him when she launched herself into his arms and fitted that gorgeous mouth to his.

Within seconds, he was lost in the taste of her, the scent, and her breath mingling with his. Both hearts hammered to the same tempo as blood ran through veins heated by desire and he gave her back kiss for kiss.

If it was a mistake, she was beyond caring as she threaded her fingers through his hair and tipped her head back to let him run his lips down her neck in a trail of fire.

Mine. The word rang in her head and was echoed as he spoke it against her lips. Mine.

Clothes trailed to the floor as she pulled him to the bedroom to give him the softness of the bed and the softness of her and they became husband and wife again in more than name only.

Amethyst awoke, yet again, to the sure knowledge that someone was watching her. When she cracked open an eye, she expected to see Tommy's familiar face its usual inch away. However, it was not the cat whose intent gaze had coaxed her from the depths of sleep.

Reid lay on his side, propped on one elbow, watching her warily.

Well, now, this is awkward was her first coherent thought.

Two distinct desires warred inside her. The first to just roll into his arms and repeat what had happened the night before, the second to jump out of bed and run away as far and as fast as she could go. She knew that the second one was not rational and that if she chose it, it would be herself she was trying to run from, not him.

No, she would not run. This time, she would stay, and this time it would be forever.

Looking at his face, she saw it was too late. He knew her well enough that he had picked up on that moment of uncertainty.

Launching himself out of bed, he pulled open the drawer and began to gather his things.

"I can't do this right now. Not when I can tell you already have one foot out the door. You don't trust me with your auras, and I get that, but it goes both ways, darlin' because I don't trust you much, either."

When he said it flat out like that, it was a slap in the face. "I'm not going to run again." She denied, but he had seen the desire for it in her eyes.

"Really? Tell me that wasn't your first thought this morning."

"I can't tell you there wasn't a moment of panic, but I'm over it now. Go ahead and leave if that's what you want. You owe me the payback. But I'm not going anywhere."

"See, that's what I'm talking about. You think I'm looking for payback? For petty revenge? Payback is the last thing I want or need, and if that's what you think of me, this isn't going to work. It's never going to work."

"So go." In a minute, she would turn into a sobbing puddle of pain.

"I made one stupid mistake, wasn't walking out on me punishment enough?"

He was right, and she knew it. The woman she wanted to be would admit it, make things right and move on to live the life of her dreams with him—have babies with him—but like Galmadriel had said, some part of her always stayed locked away keeping her from totally trusting anyone. It was why she struggled with controlling her new level of abilities, and it was why she would probably end up alone.

Amethyst looked away to keep him from seeing the truth in her eyes. More than anything, she wanted him—the life he offered—and yet, irrational though it was, the fear of deception had crawled its way inside her again and would not let go.

Frustrated, he spoke sharply, "Look at me. At least have the decency to look me in the eye this time and tell me you don't want me. I refuse to sneak out the door while you're not looking."

No response; she couldn't turn her head and just watch him walk away. Not and survive. That tiny voice in the back of her head whispered, "See? I told you he couldn't be trusted." That it was complete fiction seemed not to matter.

Softer now, "Look at me, please."

She owed him that much so she did as he asked.

"I see you, and I accept you—the whole package, fears, flaws, purple, auras and all—and if I walk out that door, it will be by your choice, your lack of trust."

No words could come when there wasn't enough breath to speak when her heart was breaking. Cursing herself, she remained silent, but tears streamed down her face.

It nearly killed him to see that she wasn't going to tell him to stay. He laid the divorce papers on the table, took one last, long look, then turned and walked out the door.

CHAPTER TWENTY-TWO

The door closed behind Reid and Amethyst completely dissolved. The divorce papers lay on the table where he had left them, and she could see their aura full of the red, and pulsing pain he had felt when he signed them.

With everything inside her, she wanted to call him back. The life she wanted—full of love and family—rested entirely with him. There would be no one else for her. If only she could have stifled that small voice inside that insisted it was all an impossible dream.

"Well, that was stupid." Estelle pulled no punches.

Amethyst, nerves on edge, rounded on the uninvited visitor. "I don't remember asking for an opinion." She replied.

"Doesn't mean you won't get one." Estelle remained unintimidated. One of the perks of being a ghost was that she was pretty much impervious to any physical threat. She planned on speaking her mind, and there was nothing Amethyst could do to stop her.

"By all means, then. Unload some wisdom on me." Her rolling eyes and sarcastic tone were both ignored because Estelle read despair in every part of Amethyst's body from her hunched posture to her pale face and trembling hands.

"Reid accepts your auras. He can be trusted with them." The words were sharp, cutting into already sensitive nerves like knives through butter.

"That's ridiculous." Amethyst scoffed.

"Is it?" Estelle gentled her voice as Amethyst stood to pace around the room, her steps moving her through the small space rapidly. "What evidence to the contrary has he given you since he came here?"

"Well, he—he…" Now that she thought about it, nothing concrete came to mind. "I just know." The words halted her pacing and sounded flimsy, even to her.

"He what? Apologized for being young and callow? And for not understanding exactly what he had asked of you? What a horrible young man!" It was Estelle's turn to drip sarcasm. "He confessed that he hadn't signed the divorce papers because he still loved you and that he waited for you for three years. I think you did the right thing by cutting him loose. He's a monster. You're well rid of him."

"No, he's not. He's everything a woman could ask for. Constant and loving and I'm an idiot for letting him go. Are you happy now?" Amethyst sneered at her own foolishness.

"Are you?" The sympathy in Estelle's eyes was enough to deflate Amethyst's anger, leaving nothing behind but misery and pain.

"Of course not." She had one of those moments where scenes from her life flashed before her eyes. Waking up on the ground with a new sense of vision, seeing the sidelong glances in school as her popularity vanished, and worse, seeing that same look in the mirror as she struggled to make sense of the unexpected change in her life.

Somehow, by internalizing the reaction of others to her gift, she had deluded herself into thinking that acceptance came from understanding and that anyone without the same gift would be unable to understand her. None of that was true or real.

"But, it's too late. He's gone. Probably halfway home by now and he made his position pretty clear, he signed the divorce papers."

"Did he, now?" Amethyst frowned at the humor she perceived in Estelle's tone. "Have you looked at them?"

"Well, no."

"I suggest you do so."

The offending documents still lay where he'd left them on the table, so she snatched them up and began to leaf through the pages. On every line where he was supposed to sign his name, he had written instead:

I love you until death do us part.

"He's at Hayward House with Tyler. Have you forgotten he's to be the best man at the wedding?"

Amethyst slumped on the sofa, dropped her head into her hands and spoke, her voice muffled by her fingers, "How does this change anything? I'm still the same hot mess I was before. Worse, even, because I still can't always control what I see. Did you know that dog pee gives off an aura?"

Estelle couldn't resist. "Is it yellow?"

"Very funny." More eye rolling.

"What did the angel say? I presume you've asked her for suggestions."

"Ha. Galmadriel is worse than Julius. *There will be three tests, and you must accept your gift.*" She imitated the stentorian tone the angel most often used. "I already did, or I wouldn't have it, would I?"

Estelle declined to answer.

"Is this one of those moments where Whitney Houston should be singing about learning to love myself in the background as I have an epiphany about how I'm not a bad person after all?"

"Something like that."

"That's total bull, and you know it. I've never thought there was anything wrong with me just because I can see something that most other people can't. I'm not a bad person, just different."

"What makes you so different? Gustavia has learned to see auras, and so has Tyler. Countless other people see them." It was a simple question with no condemnation; Estelle truly

176

wanted to understand.

"Seeing them is not the same as being able to manipulate auras. There is a lot of responsibility that comes along with being able to change a person's energy patterns."

"I see."

"Do you? People come to me with bits of old trauma blocking their energetic bodies. I can remove the blocks, but I have to think about how they came to be there in the first place and whether the person needs those blocks to deal with what happened to them. Galmadriel said my ability to heal would increase. What if I screw up? Do the wrong thing, and someone gets hurt?"

Her explanation gave Estelle a lot to think about. With a better understanding of just how much weight the young woman carried when it came to her gift, she began to see why Amethyst tended to hold back in her relationships.

After a moment of contemplation, she clarified, "What I am getting from this conversation is that it is not a matter of Reid's acceptance but of his understanding your sense of responsibility."

She had never thought of it in that light, but hearing Estelle say the words showed Amethyst the truth behind them. "I suppose that is one way to look at it."

Estelle asked the obvious question, "Have you ever explained any of this to him? To anyone?"

"I think my mother gets it, but no, I don't think I ever put it into words before. I'm not even sure I understood it myself until right now. I think I've been quite stupid."

Amethyst felt a sense of release as though a weight that she had never known she carried just simply vanished. Peace washed over her in a flash of bright light and warmth.

Bong. The bell dinged just as Galmadriel's voice sounded, "To truly accept power, one must first understand power. This was the second test."

The whistling wind smelled of snow and coursed through the trees to strip the last few clinging leaves and send them swirling toward the lake. Huddled on the couch, Amethyst pulled a colorful quilt around her shoulders and wondered what she should do next.

Having had an epiphany, even one that helped her pass the second test, had not really changed her situation. It was one thing to know what had been going wrong in her life and quite another knowing what to do to fix it.

Eyes closed, she relaxed into meditation.

Habit quickly took her back to the pleasant meadow that felt as comfortable and familiar to her as home. Breathing rhythmically, she pictured sun-drenched grass in that startling tender green of spring. Soft, warm air brushing against her face, stirring her hair and teasing her senses with the smell of spring. Soft mud oozing between her bare toes. Bees buzzing through the fragrant air to plunder the sweetness from tender blooms.

It was the most relaxed she had felt in weeks. No fighting to see through a miasma of shifting colors, just peace as the tension flowed out of her to take refuge in mother earth.

Walking through the waking dream, she lost herself in the sights and sounds until unexpectedly; she came upon a mirror standing alone in the grass.

The mirror revealed a different version of herself than the one she had been looking at for the past three years. Jane stared out at her from the polished glass; Amethyst glanced down and saw the ring on the reflection's left hand before raising her eyes back up to that Jane's face. What she saw there told a story of pain and sadness. This was the moment when she had turned and walked away from her marriage; the moment she would always remember as the rejection of a negative situation. Now, looking at a static image of herself frozen in time, she saw more. She saw that it was not Reid she had turned away from, but herself.

Protection. That's what she'd told herself it was for. That litany in her head that said, "No one will ever hurt me like that again," and it didn't matter that he had never meant to hurt her. She had been the one to build those walls, to lock parts of herself inside. At the time, it had been the only way she knew to get through—to keep moving when all she wanted to do was curl into a ball and cry.

This was what the angel had been talking about.

No, she had not accepted—not fully—that someone could love all the parts of her, especially the part that could see so deeply into them, so she had labeled herself as *other*, marked her ability as dangerous, and then never committed to it completely.

Now the image changed. It was her, as she was right now, in the glass. Leaning forward, she looked closely to see that shadow of sadness still lingering around the eyes, in the slightly stiff posture and defensive stance. This woman was a charlatan who prided herself that she practiced her true calling while, all the time, holding back.

Finally, a new image appeared. This one confident and strong. This one showing her the one thing she had never been able to see—her own aura. It was a balanced, powerful blend of color that pulsed with an otherworldly light. As she stared into the mirror, that aura reached out and enveloped her—just for a moment—bringing with it the promise of a life lived in truth.

Yes, this was her true image, her calling and her destiny. Yes.

The dinging of the bell signifying she had passed the final test vibrated through her body and soul as if she stood in the nexus of a thousand churches.

Galmadriel spoke, "To understand the self, one must look without prejudice. This was the third test."

CHAPTER TWENTY-THREE

Stalking back into Hayward House, Reid resisted the urge to slam the door but punched the alarm buttons with unnecessary force before searching out Tyler who was working in his office.

Busy at his computer, Tyler looked up as Reid slumped into a chair, kicked his feet out, and let loose a stream of invective about "that woman."

"Tell me how you really feel." His comment netted Tyler a scowl.

"You really want to know? I love her. That woman is absolutely ridiculous, and I love her anyway. She's hot and cold and I know I did something stupid one time but how long do I have to pay for that? She ran off without a word. Not a goodbye, nothing. And she thinks I can't handle her auras. I'm sleeping on the tiniest couch in the universe to make up for it. Well, I'm done. You hear me? Done."

That was a load of something most often found where bulls grazed in fields, and Tyler knew it. "Did you tell her that?"

"Yes, I did. And then I walked out."

"So you left her unprotected?"

"No, she has a group coming in for a guided meditation class today, and Julius said Logan was gone for the time being. I hung around long enough to see three carloads of clients arrive, she's safe enough for now, and I'll go back before everyone leaves because I am so obviously not done. But I'm going to give her the silent treatment." His jaw jutted out as if he expected an argument. "In the meantime, find me something productive to do."

Tyler appraised him for a moment. "You ever do any historical research for insurance? I'm running searches through multiple sources, but since we only have his first name and a possible family affiliation to work from, it isn't going well. Basically, I've got nothing."

Reid walked around to the back of Tyler's chair, looked over his shoulder at the computer screen.

The browser was open to a popular site for tracing ancestral history; search results were minimal. Tyler outlined his progress so far. "Tracing Logan's family history hit a dead end earlier than I expected. All the records on his father's side were destroyed by fire in 1872 which would have been at least one generation after Billy, possibly two."

"According to Julius, old Billy went to sea on a merchant ship, do you think there would be any records of that ship in naval history books."

"Now that's an idea." Without elaborating further, Tyler began tapping away at his keyboard.

"What?"

"Naval records. I'm pulling up a list of museums along the coast. We'll split the list, make a few calls, see what we can learn about the *Indestructible* and I will see if there are other places to access merchant ship records."

The first thing Reid learned about this type of research was that curators of naval museums loved to talk about anything related to the sea. It took five calls and three epic stories before he found the first glimmer of hope. Harry, the owner of a small museum, remembered reading about the *Indestructible* in some musty old record books. Promising to track them down, scan, and email what he found, the enthusiastic man was delighted to help. Reid flashed Tyler a thumbs up and waited for the other man to finish listening to another long yarn. Finally, Ty laid his phone down and crossed the number off his list.

"You found something?" He asked in a hopeful voice. Normally, he would have loved listening to tales of terror on the high seas with storms and swashbuckling pirates, but today, he had no patience for them.

"Looks like it." Reid gave Tyler the rundown then there was nothing left to do but wait.

When Reid stepped into the kitchen to grab a drink, two of the three resident females eyed him with enough intensity to make him squirm while the third listened just as intently. At this point, he figured he had two choices, let them keep staring at him like he was wearing his skivvies on the outside and brazen it out or grab a drink and run out of there like they were on fire. The second option sounded best. He never got the chance.

"Reid. Have a seat. Let's talk."

This sounded like the worst idea ever, but since he was too manly to throw the bottle of water as a distraction and run for his life, he warily dropped into a chair determined to bluff his way through whatever was to come.

Gustavia crossed her legs, leaned back, and appraised him before speaking to Kat, "They slept together, she got cold feet, he finally got tired of apologizing, lost his temper, and ended up here. That's my bet. Kat, you in?"

"Nah. I'd say you pegged it, nothing to bet against."

How did they know?

"She call you already?" That had to be it.

Julie answered, "No. Amethyst keeps things locked inside until she gets them sorted out for herself, even when she should be leaning on her friends. Comes from being let down in the past." The rebuke was mild, yet its barb slid home and poked his anger back to full flare.

"Ever stop to think she might have let me down, too? Sneaking away like a thief in the night without even a goodbye? Trust goes both ways, ladies, and mine was just as shattered as hers was. Did she ever stop to think about how I might feel? I came home to an empty house."

"She broke your heart." Kat's words were spoken quietly and accompanied by her reaching out to find his arm and give it a squeeze. It took a moment for him to register the empathy behind them, but once he did, all his anger dissolved leaving nothing behind but misery.

"Totally."

Gustavia reached across the table to pat his hand. She too could always be counted on to provide a bit of empathy. "Did you tell her that?"

"She doesn't want to talk about it. I thought that after last night," he confirmed Gustavia's assessment, "she might open up so we could have an honest conversation, find some resolution. Instead, she acted like she wished nothing had happened, so I yelled at her and walked out." The words sounded defensive because they were.

"You going back?" If he said no, Julie would send Tyler up the hill to make sure her friend was safe. Or even better, she would send Zack to drag her back here for the duration.

He ran a hand through his hair then rolled his eyes. It was a gesture of impatience. "Not much choice is there? I love her. I have to protect her even if that is the only thing she lets me do."

"Want some advice?" This from Kat who had, maybe, the most insight and the least experience to draw from.

"Wouldn't that be breaking some kind of female code? Fraternizing with the enemy?"

"You love her. I love her. How does that make us enemies? Do you want the advice or not?" Kat rarely spoke so firmly.

"Yes, please." He chanced a look at Julie who shrugged before turning his attention back to Kat.

"Then answer this question. Did you do everything you possibly could to find her after she left? Or did you hit a couple walls then give up and throw yourself a pity party because she hurt you?"

That was exactly what he had done, and it was nothing to be proud of.

Three years of feeling sorry for himself, of insisting he was the more injured party had netted him what? Three lonely years. Not worth it.

He looked at the table and mumbled something. Kat's voice softened, "Women want a man who will fight for them even when they've done something stupid. Actually, especially when they've done something stupid." Reid's head shot up.

"You're not completely against me?"

"Don't be an idiot. I think you seem like a pretty decent guy. You hold up pretty well under pressure. Bit thick sometimes, but your intentions are good. She never stopped loving you. Amethyst needs to know you'll always fight for her—even when it's her you have to fight."

Speculating, Gustavia judged the look on his face and came to the conclusion he thought Kat wrong. Catching Julie's eye, she waggled an eyebrow and began to run Reid through the gauntlet.

"What are your intentions for our Amethyst?"

His eyebrows shot up. "My intentions? She's my wife, and I intend to keep it that way."

"And you're willing to do whatever it takes?" Kat asked.

Gustavia nodded, "Good answer. Julie, do you have any questions for this young man before we decide whether he is a suitable match for our girl?"

"Are you able to provide for her?"

"In the manner to which she has become accustomed," Gustavia added.

"You know I'm between jobs right now, but I have savings and a very good resume."

As an aside, Julie told him, "You should talk to Tyler about that."

"I already did, and he brushed me off."

"Talk to him again." At his skeptical look, she ordered, "Just do it."

"But first, go back to Amethyst and plant your flag."

"He already did that last night," Gustavia smirked.

"I was trying to use a guy analogy—you know, stake your claim, mark your territory—and not by peeing on her."

"Listen to them; they've given you good advice," Estelle spoke from behind him, and to his credit, he didn't even jump. "Saved me having to do it. Dealing with one of you a day is enough for me. Now, go. She's there alone, her appointments for the day canceled."

Reid jumped up and made for the door. "There's no danger from Logan, he's still in the city, but I'm going to go back and keep an eye on her until you get there," Estelle assured him.

"Thanks," he called back over his shoulder.

Estelle said, "They're going to be fine now that you put a bee in his bonnet, to use a female analogy" and with a smile, she vanished while the three women tried to picture Reid in a bonnet.

CHAPTER TWENTY-FOUR

One deep breath followed another, then another. Inch by inch, Amethyst relaxed into her own skin feeling comfortable there for the first time in weeks. Right now, in this exact minute, she was just Amethyst—not a daughter, not a wife, not a friend, or a lover and especially, not a reader. There were no demands or complications. Tommy, sprawled across her lap, purred at the top of his lungs and rubbed his forehead against one hand while she used the other to comb her fingers through his soft fur.

When he rolled over to present his fuzzy, white belly, she refused to rub him there.

"Oh no, I'm not falling for that again. You get scratchy when I touch your tummy."

She sensed Reid's presence before she heard his key turning in the lock. That talk—the one she had been avoiding—was coming and this time she was ready.

He strode through the door, and her heart sped up to pound in her chest. It helped that he looked as nervous as she felt; it leveled the playing field. Still snuggling with Tommy, Amethyst waited for Reid to speak first.

He sat down on the edge of the sofa, rested his elbows on his knees, and stared straight ahead.

"I found you twice during that first year you were gone."

Now, that surprised her.

"I had no idea you were stalking me."

He shrugged. "Stalking might not be the right word. I was missing you so much and then when I saw you the first time in Arizona..."

"In a community of aura readers," she interrupted.

"When I saw you," he repeated impatiently, it was hard enough to get the words out without her commentary, "I thought—well, she's moved on. So, I went back home. A few more months went by, and I had to try again."

"What happened that time?"

"Truth? By that time, I was sunk so deeply in feeling sorry for myself that seeing you made me angry and defensive so I crawled into that self-pity and lived there."

"Yeah, I know that place; I lived there awhile myself."

"Why didn't we fight for each other? I loved you then, I love you now, but we blew it. Both of us did."

She reached out to lay a hand on his shoulder, "We were young and stupid."

"And what about now? Are we still stupid?" He knew what he wanted even if she was still unsure. "You know what? Don't answer that question." Reid stood then reached down to pull her into his arms. What he offered her now was not passion, though that always simmered below the surface, but comfort and support.

"Reid, why did you come here?"

"To protect you since you refuse to do the sensible thing."

"No, I mean why did you come to Oakville in the first place?"

"To visit a friend, clear my head and make some life decisions." That fate had stepped in and brought her back into his life was, he felt, evidence that he was where he was supposed to be.

"And you really had no idea I was living here?"

"No, none. It was kismet."

"I passed the third test." She changed the subject.

"How do you feel? Why didn't you say something right away?"

"I feel fine. In control of my ability again. Reid, there's no going back, now. My gift helps people, and I will never turn it off again. I doubt I could even if I wanted to."

There it was again. Would she ever forgive him for asking that one stupid question? He felt utterly defeated. Now he was sure she would never get past that moment, and no matter how much they loved each other, they had no future.

"That's wonderful news, I'm happy for you." He shuttered his emotions with an effort. This conversation was over. "If you don't mind, I'd like to take a shower and then I have some work to do." Without waiting for an answer, he strode from the room, and in a moment, she heard the shower come on.

She was still sitting on the sofa when he passed back through the room on his way to the kitchen where he booted up his laptop and, ignoring her thoroughly, opened his email.

Harry had come through. Attached to his email were several scanned documents mentioning the *Indestructible*. When he got a look at the final document, Reid sucked in a breath and grabbed his phone.

"Ty, I think I've got a name. William Sanford. I'm forwarding the information to you now."

He chatted with Tyler for a few more minutes, then scrolled down the list to open an email from that headhunter. He had to give the man credit for persistence. Explaining his desire to work in the non-profit sector, Reid replied and attached his resume. Maybe it would come to nothing, but at the moment, he saw no reason not to find out.

The minute the words left her lips, Amethyst regretted them. Over and over again during these past few weeks, he had supported her; even to the point of lending his strength so she could use her ability to find Gustavia. What had possessed her to bring up that particular topic at that particular moment? She should have known he would take it as an indictment even if she had only meant to indicate the finality of her actions.

He had every right to freeze her out like this. With no idea what to do next, she decided to risk a peek at his aura. Whatever she had expected to see, the wall of whiteness that met her eyes came as a total shock. White was a color she often associated with purity; it was why a baby's aura was predominantly white for the first few months. Reid was no baby and based on his performance the night before, she could attest that he had plenty of impure thoughts.

Maybe it was some type of shield.

"Reid…" she began.

"Not now, Amethyst. I'm busy." His answer was short and politely spoken, but his voice was colder than an ice cube. Well, she deserved that.

All evening he remained polite but distant. When she went into the kitchen to make dinner, he gathered up his laptop and relocated back to the sofa. Minutes spun out as the uncomfortable silence grew longer, larger, heavier. It pressed down on Amethyst until she felt it might crush her.

In the end, Amethyst retreated to her bedroom, ostensibly to read but her brain flatly refused to process any words, and she turned out the light. She knew sleep would not come easy as she listened for his movements in the other room.

CHAPTER TWENTY-FIVE

It was the day of the solstice and almost time to leave for Hayward House when the teapot started to whistle. The sound got on Reid's nerves in under a second, and he yanked it off the heat to silence the noise. Days spent trying to avoid each other in the small space had shortened his temper.

Amethyst threw him a dirty look, turned sideways to ensure their bodies did not touch and pushed past him to make tea in a travel mug. She had no idea if Reid planned to go with her or not, but when she pulled her coat from the closet and started for the door, he followed.

During the short ride to Hayward House, the silence was almost painful. Reid drove carefully but quickly as though he wanted to spend as little time alone with her as possible. She stared out the window.

The two of them walked through the door. Reid, with a nod to Julie, peeled off to find Tyler.

"Whoa. What happened? The temperature dropped ten degrees in here. Did you two have a fight?"

"Not exactly but I can't get the taste of purple ballet flat out of my mouth."

Arm in arm, Gustavia, and Kat entered the room. One look at Amethyst's face had Gustavia offering a consoling hug.

"What happened?"

"I'm an idiot; I said something stupid and blew it with him. Let's just get this done. Do we know what to do with those prisms yet?"

"No." Julie sighed. Julius had taken to popping in every two hours for the past few days to ask that same question.

After Amethyst passed by on her way upstairs, Julie and Gustavia exchanged a look, and Kat murmured, "So much tension."

Julius and Estelle were waiting near the window while Tyler fitted the first prism into the wire holder in the hidden panel they had already found. Julius, as always, appeared disgusted by his enforced silence, stood watching them avidly. Prevented from helping by whatever force that governed his particular slice of the afterlife, his agitation was evident.

Estelle, as she had the previous two times, offered to lend Kat her eyes and while the others watched, combined her essence with the medium.

"What do we do now?" Reid asked the group. Being part of the crowd had diffused enough of the tension that his stress level dropped back to a more normalized level. He even managed a smile.

"We have six more prisms and time of day. It is probably safe to assume the prisms need to all be in place by that time. Am I right, Julius?" Tyler gave Julius his version of a mock stink-eye, ignored the ghost's returning glare, then turned to his notes to read aloud the writing from the chandelier.

Glass can reflect, or it can bend light. 3:15

"The prisms bend the light. That much we know, and we have one already in place so I'd assume we need to find the rest of the holders for them."

"Amethyst knows a bit about light." Reid suggested, "Maybe with her new abilities she can read the window's aura or something."

Everyone turned expectantly toward Amethyst who hid her surprise at his unsolicited show of support. It couldn't hurt to look. After so many days of trying to control her vision enough to feel normal, it was a bit weird to release that control. After a minute or so, she was able to touch the well of power deep inside and focus on the light.

"There." She pointed toward a spear of clear glass with a circular lens in the center. It rested in a gap between the largest concentration of darker glass that made up the branches.

"Where? I don't see anything." Gustavia stared up at the glass.

"Right there. See that section between those two branches? Let Kat have a go at it with her magic fingers. If there's any kind of hidden doodad, she's the best one to find it."

It was the right call because that was exactly what Kat did. She closed her eyes and ran her fingers carefully over the section of the window that Amethyst indicated. The place where that section of glass was joined felt different from the rest of the leading. It was rougher, wider, and oddly, softer. Using the nail of her index finger, she scratched at the area.

"This section of leading is soft, it feels like clay." Kat held up her finger to show bits of something stuck under her nail.

"Hang on." Reid walked over to the desk, opened the top drawer, and pulled out a small implement that had a hard plastic handle and a hook on the end. "I found this in here the first day." He used the hook to scrape away the soft material. Underneath the fake leading, he was surprised to find a triangular-shaped bit of wire on a tiny, spring-loaded hinge. With more cleaning, a flick of his finger snapped the holder into place. "Pass me one of those prisms." He reached out to Finn who was holding them. It slid into the holder easily and fitted itself against the length of the clear glass. "Okay. Now what?"

"I guess we look for five more holders." Julie thought that was obvious. "Kat, can you check the rest of the window?"

Kat ran her hands over the rest of the leading. "Nothing here."

"Then they must be elsewhere in the room. Spread out and look around."

After a moment, Finn pointed to what looked like a

decorative area on the chandelier in the center of the room. "There, I think that's one."

"Over here, there's another one." Tyler pointed to one of the top corners of the mirror frame.

"I've got one." Gustavia fitted in a prism.

"And one here," Julie called out.

Amethyst held the final prism, it was two minutes before the indicated time, and they were coming up empty.

"Amethyst, can you check the room again?"

She stood in the center of the room, focused, and turned slowly in place. Though each of the auras around the already-found holders showed clearly, she saw no others. On a hunch, she walked through the door and onto the balcony that overlooked the living room. Directly in front of her hung another elaborate chandelier adorned with crystals and prisms. She spun and looked back toward the room she had just left.

From this vantage point, she saw it. A glimmer at the top of the door frame. "Got it." With seconds left to spare, she reached into a tiny, nearly invisible crevice, hooked the holder into position with her fingernail, and slid the prism into place.

"Now what?" She asked.

Before anyone could answer, the sun reached the correct position and slipped, magnified through the lens set into the clear glass section. Light speared into the center of the prism in its holder in the upper part of the window sent a shaft toward the prism attached to the frame, which, in turn, flashed toward the one in the middle of the room. From there the light arrowed through each prism toward the one in the doorway which directed the beam into the lighting fixture hanging above the living room. As it passed through the suspended prisms and crystals, the arc of brilliance played across the body of the fixture and a shadow image formed on the blank, facing wall.

It was another tree.

"What the...?" Tyler shook his head.

"No, wait. I've seen that before." Gustavia bumped her fist

against her forehead. "Jules, where have we seen that tree? It's so familiar."

"In the kitchen."

"The plaque over the old fireplace." Tyler was the first one down the stairs though he was followed closely by the rest of the men while the women maintained a more leisurely pace.

When Amethyst walked in, they were already poking and prodding at the plaque in the hope of triggering whatever mechanism Julius had hidden within it.

"Ammie, what do you see? Anything?" Tyler asked.

With a quirk of a smile, Amethyst declined to answer, walked to the utensil drawer, pulled out a butter knife, and used it on the four corner screws that held the plaque to the wall. "Yeah, I see that the thing is screwed to the wall, sometimes things are just as simple as they seem." Her words seemed to hold extra meaning as she caught Reid's eye.

Behind the decorative image was a section of plaster that looked different from the rest of the wall. "Sorry Jules, hope this isn't the good silver," and Amethyst jammed the butter knife into the wall. The plaster was soft and crumbly. A quick twist of the wrist and she pried out a piece, then used her fingers to yank out the rest. Behind the softened plaster was a small cavity.

"Julie, you should do the honors." Amethyst stepped back to let the other woman pull out a sheaf of papers and dog-eared journals.

"Those are my notes." Julius, released by whatever force had silenced him, was able to speak. "I'm sorry they're not especially valuable."

"May I see them?" Finn asked. As he leafed quickly through the documents, he thought Julius might not be the best judge of their value. At just a quick glance, he recognized several designs that were ahead of their time.

Respectfully, he addressed the spirit, "With some modification, there are several applications for your work. I think you underestimate its value." To Tyler and Julie, he said, "We'll talk later about those ideas we discussed before?"

"Of course."

The ride back home that evening was just as silent as the one that morning had been. Amethyst focused on the star-lined sky in an attempt to ignore the thick atmosphere between them. Before the car had come to a full stop, she was out the door and down the path.

By the time Reid walked through the door, she was already in the bedroom with the door closed.

Keeping her at arm's length had seemed like a good idea, but now he was beginning to wonder if he had made a mistake. Sometimes, though, the best offense was a good defense. Who said that? Some idiot who had never been in love with a woman like Amethyst. He would have bet on it.

Reid kicked off his shoes and stretched out on the sofa, fully clothed—as far as he could, anyway—and punched his pillow into what he hoped was a more comfortable configuration. As he had every night since then, he concentrated on dragging his mind back from its endless replay of the night she had taken him in.

Punching the pillow had helped release a little of the pent up emotion but not enough. He felt like his body would explode if he didn't do something. A few long steps took him from one side of the room to the other. Not enough.

He dragged his shoes back on, tied the laces with short, vicious movements, and grabbed his jacket from the peg hook in the laundry room. A walk in the cold would do him a world of good.

Even through the closed door, Amethyst felt his intense desire to get out of the house and assumed it would be forever. She heard the click as he gently closed the door on his way out. That was it then. He was gone. She wished she could sink through the floor; disappear into the earth. As a second-best option, she yanked the covers over her head and in the relative safety of their womb-like warmth, let it all out. Each sob shook her body like a rag doll as the tears released long-suppressed emotions.

It wasn't until he scooped her into his arms, duvet and all, that she realized he had come back. More, that he was kissing away her tears as he begged her not to cry.

"Shh, baby. I'm here." Over and over, he murmured the words of comfort as she held tight. "I'm right here."

His reassurance triggered a flood of confessions.

Everything she had never told him fell from her lips in a rain of honesty revealing fears connected to her ability that she had never admitted before. The worries she faced with her clients, the mistaken feeling that no one without her same abilities could understand her.

He told her of work experiences that he had never before shared, "Every day it seemed a little easier to go along with the crowd even if I lost myself along the way. I never thought I would lose you. I should have paid more attention." He stroked her cheek.

"Me, too. I knew you were struggling to succeed at something you never wanted to do in the first place. I should have listened to your heart, not your words. Can you ever forgive me?"

His answer came in an onslaught of kisses that washed away the past as they dove into each other and the world finally righted itself and began to spin again.

CHAPTER TWENTY-SIX

Amethyst, Gustavia, and Kat worked behind the scenes to give Julie the kind of bachelorette party that would match her temperament. Not a night of drunken debauchery—just something more her style, an evening with friends—a celebration of her marriage rather than a sendoff to her freedom.

Okay, maybe a night of tipsy tomfoolery. Without male strippers.

They debated the guest list and whether a trip to the city would be better than a night on the town in Oakville. Finally, it was decided that while a trip to the city would present considerably more options, between holiday traffic and unpredictable weather patterns, it would be a logistical nightmare.

Instead, they hired a limo and hitting all their favorite local haunts, picked up more guests along the way. Tamara, the jewelry maker, climbed in last, and they hit Tassone's for pizza before the four of them took a spin across the stage for live karaoke night with the other six partygoers as backup dancers.

Each wearing a matching tee that Gustavia and Amethyst had decorated with pictures of Julie and Tyler and glittering tiaras they made quite a picture. Julie's tiara was attached to a fluttery veil and bounced behind her while she danced across the stage, microphone in hand having the time of her life.

It was exactly the right type of party. People she loved,

celebrating and having fun and in a few short days, she would be marrying the love of her life.

Toward the end of their encore, Gustavia flashed the group one of her patented mischievous looks and reached into her pocket. The LED lights she had threaded through her braids flashed to life and began to blink. It was classic Gustavia, and the crowd gave her a standing ovation.

By midnight, it was just the four of them again, hanging out at Hayward House pouring the night's last bottle of wine while they exchanged boyfriend stories.

"Toaster oven. For Valentine's day." Julie described her last gift from Logan.

"Nope, not weird enough. Bland and boring, but not weird." Gustavia judged. "Here's mine. Remember in college when I dated that guy who played the Ocarina? He went home on break and brought me back a stuffed squirrel. Not the toy kind but the kind that comes from the taxidermist. It was creepy, and I swear the eyes followed me everywhere."

"Weirdest gift I ever got from a boyfriend? It would have to be the five-year membership to the fruit of the month club. Guy was totally into his body—like more into his than mine—and all he talked about was how fruit was nearly the perfect food. I still have over two years left on the subscription." Amethyst waved her glass.

Screaming with laughter, Kat burst out, "Ammie gets man fruit in the mail."

"Ew, that sounds really dirty," Gustavia said.

"This month it was ugly fruit and red bananas."

"Oh, I stand corrected; Ammie gets ugly man fruit in the mail." Tears streamed down Kat's face as laughter doubled her over.

"Stop it, my face hurts." Julie was also in tears, barely able to breathe.

"What exactly is an ugly fruit?" Gustavia was curious.

"A big, greenish, sort of wrinkled-up looking grapefruit."

That visual image was too much for Gustavia who now joined the hysteria.

"What about Reid? Come on, he's got some kind of quirk, right?" Kat prodded.

"Kat!" At Julie's obvious surprise, Kat answered, "What? I've had zero love life, so I have to live vicariously through you guys."

"Don't lose heart," Amethyst lifted her glass in emphasis, "weddings are a great place to meet someone."

"And Reid? How's that going?" Gustavia took up the question about half out of curiosity and half to let Kat off the hook.

Shining eyes and a slightly sappy grin told the tale, but for Kat's benefit, Amethyst confirmed, "We're totally back together."

"That's wonderful news. Are you going to move back home?" This from Julie.

"We haven't talked about that yet. He's still job hunting, so I guess it depends on what he finds. My place is a bit tight for two people so even if a miracle happened and he found something he could do here, we would have to start looking for something bigger." That was a depressing thought. She loved her little home.

"Maybe it will all work out for the best." Julie's lack of concern seemed uncharacteristic and hurtful until Amethyst got a good look at her self-satisfied expression.

Gustavia looked at Julie, raised an eyebrow in question, and at Julie's triumphant nod, began to beam.

"You," Amethyst speared a finger at Julie, "you know something, and you're holding out on me." She tried to inject a note of menace into her tone, but it fell flat. Turning to

Gustavia for support, she was surprised to see a nearly identical expression on her face. Kat's, too.

"All of you? Let me in on the secret."

"Reid will be getting a job offer."

Frowning, "What kind of job? How do you know that? I don't understand."

"Finn gave us the idea when he and Gustavia first started dating. He heard we might find Julius' notes and thought that if we did, we could form a foundation to support young inventors while simultaneously finding updated uses for some of Julius' inventions. Tyler and I loved the idea, and we want Reid to become our director."

"Is that why Tyler kept blowing him off when he asked for help finding a job?"

"We were hoping to find the notes and waiting for the final appraisals on the jewels from the last cache. That way, if there wasn't going to be enough money to create a good funding base; we wouldn't get anyone's hopes up. Last week we learned that there would be more than enough money, so we decided to move forward."

"You find a new job yet?" Tyler threw the question at Reid almost as an afterthought while lining up his new toy, a digital bowling ball, for what he hoped would not be his third gutter ball in a row. It had taken only one humiliatingly awkward release of the ball before he realized that only the wrist strap tether had kept him from tossing the controller directly into the TV.

"I'm courting offers."

"Interested in one more?" Tyler deliberately kept his tone mild.

"Hit me." Reid scored a spare.

"There's a small foundation that needs a director."

"I'm listening."

"The right person would have to wear a lot of hats, especially in the beginning because it's only in the planning phase at the moment." The prospect actually made Reid's heart speed up until reality settled in and it dropped like a stone. "I probably don't have enough experience for something like that."

"If it helps, I've got an in on the hiring committee."

The game forgotten for the moment, Reid's eyebrows shot up, and then he scowled. "Then why have you been giving me the runaround every time I ask if you know of any job openings?"

Tyler only shrugged, but the look on his face made Reid picture cats and canaries. "It was all about the timing. I'll send you a copy of the mission statement and if you like what you see, the job's yours."

"How can you promise me a job if..." Finally, Reid clued in. "It's you and Julie—starting the foundation. I would be working for you?"

"With us. You would be working with us. Let me send you the MS, no strings. You read it, think about it, and get back to me." The starting salary Tyler named was reasonable.

"You're sure you don't want someone with more experience?"

"I want someone passionate about what he does. That's you. If you need to hire a consultant, in the beginning, we can work with that."

Reid held out his hand, "Send me the Mission Statement but I can tell you right now, I'm in." The two men shook on it.

After all it had taken to get to this moment, Julie should have been a quivering bundle of nerves. Instead, she was relaxed and confident, almost regal, as she walked through the golden glow of candlelight toward Tyler, her shining eyes never leaving his for a moment. If they had, she might have noticed that Amethyst was completely oblivious to anything but Reid as she communicated her love to him without speaking.

She poured her heart into her eyes, then into his as the officiant began to speak those meaningful lines. "Dearly beloved, we are gathered here…"

Reid returned her gaze with a questioning look, Amethyst mouthed, "Will you marry me?" Her heart raced as she watched the play of emotions across his face.

When he looked back at her, she could see the sheen of tears in his eyes as they locked onto hers. "Yes," then he mouthed along with Tyler as he spoke the traditional wedding vows—for better or for worse, for richer or for poorer. Amethyst followed suit as they renewed their own commitment to each other.

The next thing she heard was, "You may kiss the bride." The wedding was over, she had missed the entire thing, and she didn't care. Sorry, Jules, she thought. I'll have to catch the video.

When it was her turn to walk up the aisle behind Kat and Tyler's younger brother, Amethyst couldn't tell if her feet touched the floor until she exited the room and was in Reid's arms, laughing and framing his face in her hands.

EPILOGUE

Kat, who carried a tearful Estelle inside her, walked down the aisle behind Gustavia and took her place before turning to watch Julie enter the room. Once the ceremony ended, Estelle would have to leave because after being present for the pre-wedding preparations, her energy was flagging. Since Julius had been dead long enough that none of the wedding guests would recognize him, he took a seat at the back of the room. Kat could see him, proud face beaming, from where she stood. Julie had tried to talk him into walking her down the aisle but, knowing he was not supposed to show himself to people on that grand a scale, he declined. It was one thing to sneak in at the back of the room and quite another to parade himself down the aisle.

Watching Julie walk toward Tyler, Kat was ashamed that one of the emotions running through her was envy and even though she tried, she could not entirely shut that feeling down. It saddened her to think she might never experience this for herself. The feeling persisted throughout the ceremony and even after as she allowed Estelle the change to give Julie a hug before the spirit had to pull her energy away. When darkness settled back over her vision, she prepared to withdraw into the background as much as she could and still perform her bridesmaid duties with a smile.

It was not to be.

Anticipating Kat's plans, Gustavia had made some of her own. As soon as the dancing started, she pulled Kat from her seat. "Come on. It's time to dance."

"I don't dance."

"Tonight you do." Gustavia dragged her over to where Zack sat. "You, get out of that chair and dance with Kat. Leave the cop behind and just have some fun."

"Gustavia, let the poor man alone. I'm sure he doesn't want to dance with me." And he didn't but not for the reasons Kat had built up her mind. Shooting daggers at his sister for putting him in this position, he had no choice but to answer, "Of course I do," and take her hand.

As he reluctantly paced toward the edge of where everyone was dancing, he thought, *at least she won't see what she is stuck dancing with* and shaking his head, began to move.

If two people had ever been more self-conscious on the dance floor, Zack was sure he had never seen them. Even carrying full gear, he could outrun most perps, but dancing required rhythm and some indefinable bit of coordination that he just did not possess. His favored move was little more than shifting from one foot to the other and never in time to the music.

Kat had danced before losing her sight and enjoyed it but, now, she was always on hyper-alert in fear that she would bump into someone and cause a scene. Consequently, she tried to occupy as little space as possible, which ended up with a very similar style to Zack's only with a bit more grace and in time to the music.

Now, the thought that preoccupied her mind was what to do when the song ended. Gustavia had dragged her to Zack, and he had led her here so quickly she hadn't been able to count her steps or orient herself directionally. At this point, she had no idea how to get back to her seat, and she felt uncomfortable asking Zack. Maybe he would offer to take her back to Gustavia, or maybe she would just end up standing here like an idiot while he walked away with no idea he should.

When the song ended, and a slow number came on, Zack thanked her for the dance. Instead of walking away, though. He asked, "Another?" Kat nodded. He pulled her in close.

From her spot in the corner, Estelle smiled and faded away as she saw the thought she had planted in Zack's head take hold. There, she thought, her part in this wedding was over, time to go recharge her energy for what lay ahead.

Kat put the surge of energy bursting through her down to the fact that she wasn't used to being held in a man's strong arms. Plus, he smelled really good. She felt her face flaming red. This was Gustavia's brother, and she probably shouldn't be thinking about him that way.

"I never had the chance to thank you for your help in finding Gustavia." The words grated but he owed her them. In his opinion, their finding her had less to do with psychic phenomenon than just plain luck. That she had been in a remote enough location that luck could not explain her rescue was ignored.

"Amethyst did that, not me." If he thought he was hiding his attitude toward anything beyond the mundane behind a thin veneer of politeness, he was trying that with the wrong person because Kat easily felt his disdain for those with certain abilities.

"This situation with Ellis is beyond ridiculous. He has had a run of uncanny good luck." So, that's what he wants to call it, she thought.

"He's had some help from the other side." Her voice was dry as dust.

His snort of derision shot her head up as she readied to level him with a cutting verbal defense. The words died in her throat, though as somehow, her unseeing gaze reached his face. For a moment, her vision cleared and she found herself looking into eyes brown and warm as melted chocolate.

Made in the USA
Las Vegas, NV
27 November 2023

81639063R00118